T.J. and the Pirate Who Wouldn't Go Home

T.J. and the Pirate Who Wouldn't Go Home

Carol Gorman

AN
APPLE
PAPERBACK

SCHOLASTIC INC.
New York Toronto London Auckland Sydney

ISBN 0-590-43303-2

Copyright © 1990 by Carol Gorman. All rights reserved. Published by Scholastic Inc. APPLE PAPERBACKS is a registered trademark of Scholastic Inc.

12 11 10 9 8 7 6 5 4 3 2 1   0 1 2 3 4 5/9

Printed in the U.S.A.   40

First Scholastic printing, August 1990

For my parents, John and Marian Maxwell,
with love

1

If I hadn't been failing history, I would probably never have seen the pirate in the first place. So I suppose I owe the whole crazy adventure to Ms. Dougan.

Well, maybe I'd better start at the beginning.

My name is Timothy Joseph O'Brien, but everybody calls me T.J. I'm in sixth grade, and Ms. Dougan is my history teacher. She called me up to her desk after class the day before spring break and told me that if I didn't do something drastic to pull up my grade, I was going to fail the class. I told her that I'd really been trying. But then she pointed out that I'd fallen asleep in class twice just that week, and how could I really be trying when I was unconscious. She had me there.

So I asked her if I could work on an extra-credit project. Ms. Dougan frowned, scraped back her chair, and stood up. And I, knowing Ms. Dougan quite well after having been imprisoned in her classroom five days a week for some eight months now, immediately stepped back. I've learned that you don't mess with Ms. Dougan.

Now you're probably thinking that she's this gigantic, scary-looking witch, right? Wrong.

Ms. Dougan probably weighs all of one hundred pounds, and the top of her head reaches to about the middle of my forehead. And I suppose that if I had to be absolutely honest, I might even add that she is somewhat cute. For a teacher, that is.

So why did I take a step back? First, Ms. Dougan is known for her quick temper; and second, Ms. Dougan has a black belt in karate. And while I'd never actually seen her karate in action, I *had* seen her temper in action. And I'd heard the "attempted Dougan robbery" story hundreds of times.

It was in all the newspapers. Some guy who didn't know any better broke into Ms. Dougan's house one night about three A.M. Ms. Dougan heard a noise and walked into the living room to see him carting her digital compact disc player out the door. She grabbed the robber by the hair on the back of his head, and he dropped the disc player. When the police finally got there, they found him sprawled out on his stomach on the kitchen floor, with Ms. Dougan standing on top of him, yelling at him to shut up and quit squawking.

This last part wasn't in the papers, and maybe the story got juiced up a bit since it happened. But I'm trying to explain why I took that step back.

Anyway, Ms. Dougan frowned and walked slowly around her desk. "I don't like to accept extra-credit projects, T.J.," she said. "Too many students don't do their work all year and then want to bail themselves out at the last minute with extra credit."

"Yes, I know," I said.

There was a long pause. Then she sighed and said, "What did you have in mind?" She folded her arms in front of her and stared up at me.

"Well, I don't know exactly," I said. "Could I have a few days to think about it?"

"Okay," Ms. Dougan said, strolling back behind her desk thoughtfully. Then she planted both hands on her desk and leaned over toward me. "But this project will have to be very, *very* well done to affect your grade." She stared up at me. "Get it?"

"Got it," I said.

"Good."

I turned to leave.

"Oh, and T. J. . . ." she said, stopping me.

"Yeah?" I turned back to her.

3

"Choose a topic that interests you. Have the project ready when you return from spring break."

"Okay," I said and turned to go a second time.

"T.J.?"

I turned back.

"Don't you ever sleep at *home*? Or do you count on history class for your beauty rest?" She had a half smile on her face.

"Oh, sorry, Ms. Dougan," I mumbled. "I'll stay awake from now on. I promise."

"I'll hold you to it," she said, her eyes flashing, but still with that half smile.

"I figured you might," I said.

"God didn't give me this red hair for nothing," she said. "You may go now, T.J."

I only mention this conversation with Ms. Dougan to explain why I had to go to the library that night. I'm not all that fired up about history, in case you hadn't guessed, but I dreaded the thought of failing the course. My parents are both college professors, and they expect me not only to pass, but to pass with flying colors. You know, because of the genes and all that.

I thought I'd just look around in the history section and find a subject for my extra-credit report. I was hoping something interesting would catch my eye.

4

Nothing did.

Then I remembered that my Uncle Ainsley had an *Encyclopedia of American History.* I thought maybe I could find something quicker just by leafing through it. Worth a try, anyway, I decided as I grabbed my Lincoln Junior High jacket.

I let the library door swing shut softly behind me at the side entrance that opened onto a dark alley. It was late April, and I filled my lungs with the crisp night air.

It was very dark outside. I could see the streetlight just over the corner of Rick's Radio and TV where the alley meets Franklin Avenue. But in the shadows where I stood, I couldn't see more than a few feet in front of me. I'm not exactly afraid of the dark; I'm more afraid of what's *in* the dark. I was feeling pretty nervous about being in this gloomy place, so I started to hurry toward the streetlight at the end of the alley.

Suddenly I heard the sound of splintering glass behind me at the back of the radio and TV store. I froze right there in the middle of the alley, not daring to move.

I turned my head in the direction the sound had come from. I couldn't see anything at first, it was so dark.

But then I caught sight of something moving in the shadows by a back window. I scurried over to a big waste bin near the back of the store and ducked behind it.

CRASH! More shattering glass.

Slowly I raised my head and peered over the edge of the rusty bin. My eyes were beginning to get accustomed to the darkness. I strained to get a look at whoever was standing there whacking away at what was now probably an almost paneless window.

Then I drew in a quick breath. Maybe the dim light was playing tricks on me. I rubbed my knuckles into my eyes and stared again.

He was still there.

Standing before me in the shadows was a real-life, honest-to-gosh pirate!

I mean, he looked like every pirate you've seen in those old-time movies: He wore a crimson waistcoat and breeches, his hair was pulled back behind his neck, and he had on a hat with a tall feather sticking out of it. Hanging from his belt was a long sword, and a pair of pistols hung from a silky-looking sling over his shoulder. And to top it all off, he had a patch over his right eye!

I watched, I'm sure with my mouth wide open, as he grabbed hold of the frame around the outside of the window, hoisted himself over the sill, and disappeared into Rick's Radio and TV.

I remained motionless right where I was, trying

to decide what I should do. Of course, it made sense to run and get some help. Maybe call the police. But I have to admit, I was so curious about seeing a living, breathing pirate, that I didn't want to leave just yet. I wanted to get a better look at him.

Maybe he wasn't a real pirate, I thought. Maybe this guy was on his way to a masquerade party and decided at the last minute to break into a store. You know, identifying with his costume and all.

Just then, the pirate hopped back onto the windowsill. I ducked behind the bin just in time. I don't think he saw me.

Slowly I raised my head just enough to watch him. He was carrying something in a large box, but he got himself and his loot out of the window without any problem and jumped to the pavement.

Now I started to sweat. This pirate, or whoever he was, was the fiercest-looking human being I've ever laid eyes on. It occurred to me that staying in his near-vicinity was probably hazardous to my health.

I turned and crept, as quietly as I could, along the back wall of Rick's store. Unfortunately I didn't see the old aluminum can just in front of my right foot.

The pirate heard it, though, as it skidded down the alley.

A huge voice bellowed behind me, "I see ye, matey!" I glanced back just in time to see him pull out his sword.

I took off faster than I'd ever started a race in Mr. Masters's phys ed class. Funny how much faster you can move when you're about to be run through with a sword.

I moved swiftly in and out of the shadows, hearing the pirate's footsteps close behind. I could hear him breathing heavily as he lumbered after me.

Just then, I tripped over something in the dark and fell to the pavement.

I scrambled to my feet, but two heavy hands grabbed me from behind. The pirate whirled me around to face him, grabbing my shirt at the collar.

He thrust his face down to within inches of mine. If he'd come any closer, I'd have felt the prickly hairs sticking out of his unshaven chin.

The pirate flashed a fierce smile, displaying holes where some of his teeth should have been.

"Ye be havin' business back here, mate?" he growled.

Of course, I could very well have asked *him* the same question, but the situation being as it was, I decided against it.

"N-No," I stammered. "I'm on my way home."

The pirate let go of my shirt. "Then may I be suggestin' that ye remove yerself from these here premises before Blacky takes a real dislikin' to ye?" He patted his sword. (I didn't inquire, but I assumed Blacky was his sword.)

He didn't have to ask me twice.

I was out of that alley like a shot. I mean, we're talking *Guinness Book of World Records* stuff.

One thing I was sure of now. He wasn't just any old guy dressed up in a costume. This pirate was for *real!*

2

When you're running for your life, you're not likely to think very clearly. So I didn't bother to wonder about the pirate until I was safely home, behind locked doors.

By the time I slid the deadbolt into place and collapsed against the front door, panting and sweating, I'd made one excellent decision, however. I wasn't going to tell Mom and Dad about what I'd just seen. Actually, I didn't know at the time just how brilliant a decision that was. I was to find that out later. And I suppose, since I'm telling you the whole story, I should mention here that it wasn't hard to keep the pirate story a secret from my parents, at least the first night. They weren't home. They'd gone out to some concert or something.

I fell asleep with my light on, something I hadn't done since I was a little kid. When I finally woke up, it was morning, and sunlight was streaming through my window.

Usually, things that seem scary in the dead of night are laughable in broad daylight, when I can always come up with a reasonable explanation. I lay on my bed waiting for the reasonable explanation to occur to me.

But after twenty minutes of staring at the ceiling, I realized I was getting nowhere.

I mean, how can you explain seeing a pirate break into a radio and TV store?

So then I tried to decide what to do about it. Should I tell someone? The police?

Then I pictured myself at the police department telling my story.

"And did you get a good look at the suspect?" the police detective would ask.

"Yes," I'd say, proud of my powers of observation.

"And what did he look like?" the detective would ask eagerly.

"Well, he wore a short coat and breeches —"

"Breeches?"

"Yes. And he had a tall hat with a feather sticking out of it —"

By this time, the police detective would have stopped taking notes and would be staring at me.

"— and he carried a long sword, two pistols, and wore a patch over his right eye."

I decided I wouldn't try to imagine what the officer would say to that.

No one would ever believe my story.

Suddenly I had a thought. Of course! I jumped up from my bed. There *was* someone who might believe something as crazy as this. My Uncle Ainsley.

Uncle Ainsley is my mother's brother. He's a science professor at Cedar Springs College, where my parents also teach.

Uncle Ainsley could be described as *eccentric*. (That was a vocabulary word we learned in English this year. It means: *extraordinary, unusual, odd*. In other words, he's nuts.)

One time my parents had a party and invited a lot of teachers from the college. Apparently they "forgot" to invite Uncle Ainsley. I overheard a math professor ask my father and mother if they'd ever heard of Ainsley Weed in the science department. The guy was grinning as if he had a great story to tell about this weirdo, Ainsley. My mother turned strawberry red. My father said, "Who?" and suddenly remembering the charcoals were ready for cooking, he took my mother's arm and guided her away.

Uncle Ainsley would've hated the party anyway.

My uncle is the kind of person you can talk to about anything. Because he talks to *you* about anything. And I mean anything.

Once he told me he wanted to fly by making himself a pair of gigantic wings, attaching them to his arms, and jumping off the United City Bank, which is the tallest building in town. He'd studied birds for months, weighing dead birds he'd found (he'd hung around the next-door neighbor's cat a lot) and measuring their wings. Then he'd made calculations about how large his wings would have to be to keep him up in the air after he'd jumped off the bank.

He was all ready to try his experiment until I pointed out that he couldn't jump off the bank, because it's located downtown. What if he fell on someone, or landed in the street, or was thrown in jail for causing a disturbance?

He just rubbed his chin thoughtfully and said, "Well, I guess I'd better forget about this one."

He never mentioned it again.

But don't ever think that my Uncle Ainsley is dumb. He's one of the smartest people I know. He's an expert on history and has invented some pretty handy gadgets. He's very smart. Just a little eccentric, that's all.

Anyway, I figured if I could tell anyone about the pirate, it would be Uncle Ainsley.

I rode my bike over to his house, which is just about three blocks from mine. I found him sitting on his front porch wearing his blue terrycloth bathrobe and old brown slippers, reading the morning newspaper. What hair he had was all messed up and sticking up in the back as if he hadn't combed it since he got out of bed. He was squinting at the paper through his reading glasses.

He looked up over the glasses as I approached on the front walk.

"Well, T.J., my boy, you're up early this morning," he mumbled, nodding a welcome.

"How come you're sitting outside in your bathrobe, Uncle Ainsley?" I asked.

He glanced down at his robe and back up at me. "Why not?" he asked simply, and went back to his paper.

Just then, I heard a familiar voice sing out, "Good morning, good morning! And a beautiful day it is, too!"

I didn't need to look up to know who was calling. Only one person in the world talks that way, in a sort of nasal, chirpy, high-pitched voice. It was Mrs. Harkle from across the street. She stood on her front porch twiddling her fingers in the air, waving at us, as the breeze snatched at wisps of her dark hair.

Uncle Ainsley smiled politely and waved back. "She's certainly cheerful," he noted, keeping his voice low. "Ever since she moved here from Springfield after her husband passed on, she's been bringing me cookies and offering to tend my garden for me." He looked down at the fine crop of weeds between the tulips. "Maybe I ought to let her get at those weeds. Hire her, you know." Then, waving again and plastering this phony smile on his face, he whispered out of the side of his mouth, "But the woman drives me crazy."

Mrs. Harkle chirped from across the street, "Oh, I nearly forgot. I have something for you!"

She disappeared into her house and reappeared a moment later carrying a large, white plate. She hurried down her front walk, crossed the street, and approached us with a big smile.

Mrs. Harkle is on the plump side and has dark hair that's always done up in some fancy arrangement. I guess she missed a strand or two when she was squirting on the hairspray today, though, because, as I said before, the breeze was blowing some of it around her face. She was dressed, as usual, as if she were going to a party, in a sky-blue dress with shoes the same color.

Just then, in the middle of Uncle Ainsley's front walk, she noticed what my uncle was wearing, and she slowed her pace and laughed heartily. "Why, Ainsley Weed, you're still in your jammies!" she said and laughed some more. "Were you a sleepyhead this morning?"

Uncle Ainsley shot me a "see-what-I-mean?" look, but smiled politely.

I jumped off the porch and accepted the plate of cookies. "Would you like the plate back now, Mrs. Harkle?" I asked.

"Oh, my, no," Mrs. Harkle said, beaming. "Just keep my little china plate for as long as you like. I have plenty of them. And I certainly won't miss one, what with my living *alone* and all." This last part she said looking right at my uncle.

Uncle Ainsley murmured a thank-you at her. I guess she realized my uncle wasn't in a talkative mood, because after a moment, she took a step back, her hands clasped in front of her. "Well, I guess I'd better get back to my baking." She smiled. "Nothing smells better than cookies in the oven!" She twiddled her fingers in the air again, still beaming, and headed back down the front walk. "Toodle-oo!" she sang out over her shoulder.

"Interesting woman," Uncle Ainsley mused, looking after her and stroking his chin. "What do you suppose she wants?"

"Well, I may be wrong, Uncle Ainsley, but I think she wants *you*," I said, trying to hide the smile that I could feel creeping across my face.

Uncle Ainsley looked at me, astonished. "You don't say," he said.

He slowly got to his feet, and we walked to his front door. Then he turned to me suddenly and said, "Well, T.J., it was nice to see you. Come again soon." He started to turn away.

"Wait," I said and stopped him with a hand on his arm. "Can I come in? I'd like to talk to you."

For a long moment, Uncle Ainsley just stood there staring at me, his eyes wild and confused.

"Are you okay?" I asked.

"Oh. Well, yes." He stopped again and stared at me, looking as if he were thinking about something else.

Then he made some sort of decision and grabbed my arm and pulled me back down the porch steps. "Why don't we just walk around back," he suggested, obviously trying to sound casual.

I decided to play along. He didn't seem to want to explain what was going on.

"Okay, sure," I said.

"Now, what did you want?" he asked as we walked around the side of the house.

"Well, something happened to me last night, and I didn't know who else to tell," I started to explain.

"Yes?" he said. We were in the backyard now.

"Well, I was at the library last night. It was pretty late, and as I was leaving I heard the sound of glass being shattered in the alley. When I went to find out what was going on, I saw somebody breaking into Rick's Radio and TV." We sat down on the back steps. "I hid and watched as the guy hauled a big box out the back window."

Uncle Ainsley shook his head and said something that sounded like "tsk, tsk."

"But, Uncle Ainsley, I got a good look at the guy!" Uncle Ainsley looked directly at me. "He was a pirate, Uncle Ainsley! A *real* pirate!"

Uncle Ainsley's mouth fell open. "Oh, no!" he said, shaking his head.

"I swear to you, it's the truth," I said. "He grabbed me and told me to get lost and threatened me with his sword."

"Oh, my!" was all my uncle said. He had a strange look on his face.

"I just don't think I can tell anyone — besides you — about it," I said. "Nobody would believe me. They might even think *I* was the one who broke in or something."

"Oh, I agree with you, T.J.," my uncle said. "I don't think it would be wise to tell the police or anyone. You don't want to get into trouble, yourself." He shook his head hard from side to side.

"But it was really crazy," I said.

"It certainly sounds crazy," Uncle Ainsley agreed, now nodding up and down.

"But I know I didn't just imagine it," I said.

"No, I'm sure you didn't imagine it," Uncle Ainsley said.

"Well, how do you explain it?" I asked.

"I couldn't begin to guess," Uncle Ainsley said, looking straight at me with wide, unblinking eyes.

This conversation wasn't getting me anywhere.

"Well, thanks anyway," I said, standing up. "It was good to get this off my chest."

"Any time, my boy," Uncle Ainsley said, rising and patting me on the shoulder, smiling. "If I can ever help you again, just let me know."

I nodded, said good-bye, and started down the steps. Then I remembered something.

"Oh, Uncle Ainsley," I said, "you know that *Encyclopedia of American History* you have? May I borrow it for a few days? I need to come up with a project to save my history grade."

Uncle Ainsley looked startled, and at first I thought he'd loaned the book to someone else. But he said, "Oh, yes. Uh, wait right here, and I'll go get it."

"Oh, that's okay," I said. "Don't bother, I know right where it is."

I gently pushed past him and made my way through the old-fashioned kitchen, down the hall, and paused at the closed door to the den.

I could hear the TV inside. Uncle Ainsley was hurrying down the hall after me, saying something unintelligible. I pushed open the door and stepped in.

I gasped.

Vanna White was on TV, standing on a platform at the side of the letter boards, clapping her hands and smiling. The contestant was saying, "I can solve the puzzle, Pat! It's: HOW MUCH IS THAT DOGGIE IN THE WINDOW?"

The audience cheered.

And in front of the TV set, sitting cross-legged on the floor, gnawing on a chicken leg, was none other than the pirate himself!

3

Uncle Ainsley!" I cried out. "That's the pirate! I saw him break into Rick's last night! Who is he? What's he doing here?"

At the same time that I was saying this, Uncle Ainsley was stuttering, "N-Now, T.J., I can explain everything. J-Just settle down and —"

"PIPE DOWN, you dogs!" the pirate bellowed. We both stopped yelling and stared at the pirate, who glared at us angrily from his spot on the floor.

"Can't ye see I'm watchin' me program here?" He paused. "That's better." The pirate turned briefly back to the TV and then scratched his head, thoughtfully. "Now, Weed, get over here and tell me about this program I'm watchin'. These people are playin' a game, me thinks, and they win a treasure if they guess the puzzle, am I right?"

Uncle Ainsley stole a glance at me, cleared his throat, and said to the pirate, "Uh, well . . . yes, that, I believe, is the premise of the, uh . . . show."

"Aye, I've figured it out, then," the pirate said. He tossed the chicken leg down on the floor and wiped his mouth on his sleeve. "Got any ale, Weed?" he called back over his shoulder. He was so engrossed in the program, he didn't seem to notice when my uncle didn't answer.

I slowly turned my head to look at Uncle Ainsley. He shrugged with an embarrassed smile and said softly, "He likes television."

Uncle Ainsley beckoned for me to follow him out of the den. He carefully closed the door behind him.

"What's going on here, Uncle Ainsley?" I asked when we were in the living room.

My uncle looked frightened, like a little boy who's just been caught wiping his dirty hands on his mother's drapes.

"Sit down, T.J.," he said. "Would you like a Pepsi?"

"No," I said.

"Hot chocolate?"

"No."

"A bowl of soup?"

"No, Uncle Ainsley. Just tell me who that guy is."

"Well, T.J., it's a long, involved story," my uncle said, sitting nervously on the edge of his favorite recliner.

"I've got time," I said. "Who is he?"

"Well, he is who he appears to be," Uncle Ainsley said.

"A pirate?" I asked.

"Precisely," he said.

"A *real* pirate?"

He nodded.

"So what's he doing here?" I asked.

"Apparently, he is watching television," Uncle Ainsley said, looking serious.

"I can *see* that, Uncle Ainsley. But who is he? Other than a pirate, I mean. What's his name?"

"He is Captain Billy Mulligrew."

"Where did he come from?" I asked.

"The Atlantic Ocean, I think," my uncle said. "But I'm not completely sure about that."

"Uncle Ainsley," I said. "I didn't know there were any pirates left. Do people still dress like that?"

"Oh, no," my uncle said.

"So —" I stopped, frustrated. "I don't understand this."

"Oh, I guess I'd better clear things up for you," Uncle Ainsley said. Then he sighed. "I knew someone would find out sooner or later."

He got up from his chair and walked to the window. "You see, I've been working on a secret project for a very long time."

"You mean, like for the CIA?" I asked.

"Oh, no, no. Not anything like that," he said. "This project was a secret because I thought it best that I keep it to myself. To avoid publicity."

"What project?"

Uncle Ainsley sighed again as he stared out the window at the maple tree in his front yard. He shook his head. "You'll have a hard time believing what I'm about to say."

"Uncle Ainsley, after hearing about your plan to jump off the United City Bank and fly with wings Scotch-taped to your arms, I'll believe anything."

"I wasn't going to *tape* them to my arms," he said indignantly. "I was planning to secure the wings with heavy postal string." He drew himself up proudly. "If it's good enough for the U.S. Postal Service, it's —"

"— good enough for me," I finished with him.

Uncle Ainsley began pacing back and forth in front of his window. "Well, you see, T.J., I was working on this project that I thought could rewrite the history of this country. Imagine being able to rewrite history!" His words faded as he stopped and stared outside again, lost in his thoughts.

"Yes?" I said. "What was this project?"

"Hunh?" Uncle Ainsley started. "Oh, yes. I was telling you about my invention."

"What invention?" I asked.

"Well, the time machine, of course!" my uncle said.

I sat there and stared at him, not sure I'd heard him right. "Did you say, 'time machine'?" I asked.

"Yes, yes, the time machine." Uncle Ainsley sounded impatient. "Pay attention, my boy."

"You invented a time machine?" I asked.

"Yes, that's what I just told you," Uncle Ainsley said.

"You mean, like a machine that will take you into another period of time? You could travel back to the time of Shakespeare or George Washington?"

"To meet the father of our country!" Uncle Ainsley said solemnly.

"Can this machine take you forward in time to see what the world would be like in the year 2200?" I asked.

"Presumably," my uncle said. "But, you see, I had a slight foul-up in the system." He shrugged and looked embarrassed. "Instead of *me* going *back* in time, this other, uh, *person* came *forward* in time."

"The pirate?" I asked.

"You got the picture," he said, nodding.

"Well, where is this time machine?" I asked.

"Down in the basement," he answered.

Somehow, Uncle Ainsley's basement didn't seem like the right place for an invention as wonderful as a time machine. His basement is a dark, dusty old place, piled with boxes that are filled with stuff like photograph albums, scrapbooks, old clothes, and Christmas ornaments. There are a couple of lamps that are broken, a vacuum cleaner in need of repair and, well, you know, junk like that.

A time machine should stand in the middle of an ultra-modern science lab with sparkling clean lab equipment. The machine should be painted white with shiny chrome fixtures. And the inventor should wear a crisp white lab coat, not a blue terrycloth bathrobe and bedroom slippers.

"Can I see it?" I asked.

"Come with me," he said and led the way to the basement stairs near the back door.

We carefully descended the steps, and I say carefully, because if you're not careful, you'll break your neck with no trouble. Uncle Ainsley isn't exactly a great housekeeper. The sides of the stairs, from top to bottom, are piled with stuff. Magazines, books, bundles of newspapers that Uncle Ainsley forgot to put out for the garbage,

Pepsi bottles — all kinds of things are heaped along the pathway from the main floor to the basement.

Reaching the bottom of the stairs, he turned to his left and entered a small dark room. He flipped on the wall switch, and instantly the room was flooded with light from the fluorescent fixture hanging from the ceiling.

And there, standing in the middle of the room, was the time machine.

This time machine fitted perfectly in Uncle Ainsley's basement. It looked like a large, walk-in closet, extending from the floor to the ceiling, made entirely of metal.

But not shiny new chrome or gleaming stainless steel. This metal was red with rust and so dented that it looked as if someone had gotten mad and attacked it with a hammer. Uncle Ainsley explained why.

"This marvelous invention hardly cost me anything," he said proudly. "I picked up all of this hardware at the auto salvage yard for a song. Then all I needed was some welding equipment, which I rented from Acme Rentals for a couple of days, and then just a pinch of this and a little of that. And then, of course, some old-fashioned know-how." He smiled slyly and pointed to his head.

"Amazing," I said. I walked over to the machine and touched it carefully with my finger. "How does it work?"

"It's really very simple," Uncle Ainsley said. "First, you turn it on here." He pressed a red button and a panel slid open. I peered into the closetlike space.

The back wall of the contraption reminded me of the cockpit of a plane. It was completely covered with dials, buttons, levers, and blinking lights.

Uncle Ainsley pushed me gently into the chamber and the door slid closed behind us.

Now, I don't know how you feel about getting stuck in an elevator with no way to get out, but the idea of being in any enclosed place sets my heart racing. My palms — and the rest of my body — get very sweaty. That's exactly how I felt when Uncle Ainsley closed us inside. Also, I didn't relish the idea that my uncle could make a tiny mistake and zoom us back into the Middle Ages or forward into World War III.

"Uncle Ainsley, can you get us out of here?" I asked, trying not to let the panic show in my voice.

"Of course, of course," he said, with a wave of his hand. "Now once inside, you proceed to the instrument panel here."

"Uncle Ainsley, will you please open the door to this thing?" I asked.

"In just a minute," he said impatiently. "Now, the second step is to flip on this switch, turn this dial to the left two times around, set the date we want in the past or the future on the chronometer, press the black button, and pull this lever. And *voilà!* Time travel!"

Uncle Ainsley turned to me triumphantly. "But of course, I won't do that now, heh-heh, because we want to stay here, don't we?"

"Uncle Ainsley," I said, feeling as if I were about to suffocate, "please let me out of here."

But my uncle didn't even hear me. He was too wrapped up in his speech about the invention.

"Of course, I can send Captain Billy back, too," he said. "When the time comes, I just spin the dial twice and — oh — do you see that wooden rack above your head?" He pointed to a small flat structure above us. It had a crack down the middle. "I grab hold of that and pull very hard. Then I have five seconds to get out of the machine so that only the captain goes back to 1699." He smiled. "And that's all there is to it."

Uncle Ainsley looked serious a moment. "But I must be very careful to do all the right things. For instance, if I forget and push this lighted button, or if I turn this particular knob," he pointed to a round disc mounted on a square of ceramic tile, "I could shoot Captain Billy into a timeless void from which he would never escape. He'd wander forever, lost in time."

"Uncle Ainsley," I murmured.

"Just a minute," he said, frowning. "Don't interrupt, my boy. You are a part of something big here. History is being made in this basement." Then he smiled. "I wanted to make sure that I didn't forget how to send Billy back in time. I don't know if you've ever noticed, but sometimes I can get a tad forgetful. So I made up this little rhyme to help me remember. It goes like this:

'Spin this device around twice
for the trip that is nice.
Then pull the rack with a crack
to track the time back.

But turn the dial on the tile
and the pirate you will rile.
For the light on the right
sends him ever out of sight.' "

He grinned at me. "Clever, don't you think?"

I grabbed my uncle by the shoulders and began shaking him. "Uncle Ainsley, I just want to get *out* of here! This is making me CRAZY!"

"No problem, my boy," he said. "Why didn't you say so?" He touched a blue button on the panel. Instantly the door slid open, and I threw myself out of the closet and onto the concrete basement floor.

It took me several minutes to stop breathing so fast and get myself pulled back together. I wouldn't have gone back inside that chamber for anything.

After awhile, I started thinking clearly again.

"Uncle Ainsley, why don't you send the Captain back now, since he's getting into so much trouble?"

"This is where the human element comes into play," Uncle Ainsley said, rubbing his chin. "You see, Captain Billy was shot into the twentieth century quite abruptly. He came from the 1690s. At that time, people didn't have the, well, the comforts that we have now. And Captain Billy rather likes the style of living in this century. He doesn't *want* to go back."

"Can't you just send Captain Billy back anyway?" I asked. "After all, he broke into Rick's store last night. Isn't that reason enough to boot him back?"

"I wish it were that simple, my boy," Uncle Ainsley said, and he collapsed on the basement stairs. "You see, the day I first mentioned sending

Captain Billy back was the same day I drove him in the car for the first time and bought him a Big Mac."

"Yes?" I said, not understanding.

"He was so excited by the ride in a motor car that carried us along the street without being pulled by horses, and he so loved that darned burger, that when I suggested that he might like to go back to his friends on the pirate ship," Uncle Ainsley paused, groping for the right words, "he, well, he went rather berserk. He threatened me with his cutlass and said he'd cut me to ribbons. Naturally I dropped the subject."

"Well, how long has Captain Billy been here?" I asked, remembering how comfortable the pirate looked with the TV upstairs.

"Four days," said Uncle Ainsley gloomily.

"He sure seems to have learned a lot in four days."

Uncle Ainsley sighed. "He's a fast learner. Just because he's from 1699 doesn't mean that he's dumb. In fact, the man is really rather crafty." Uncle Ainsley looked thoughtful. "Yes," he said. "Like a fox."

"What's he been doing since he got here?" I asked.

"Well, when he first arrived, I spent all my spare time getting him acquainted with modern living. I was so afraid someone would discover my secret. I thought I'd better teach him how to get along in the modern world while I figured out how to send him back to 1699. He was fascinated with all these inventions that were new to him. I didn't worry about him leaving the house for the first day, because all he wanted to do was play with my food processor and flush the toilet."

"Flush the toilet?" I asked.

"*Everything's* new to him!" My uncle ran his hand over the top of his head, smoothing his few hairs. "I didn't want him to learn how to drive the car — can you imagine the trouble he'd get into? — but when I took him out that one time, he was watching me pretty carefully as I drove. I just hope I can send him home before he figures it out!"

"Uncle Ainsley, we've got to send him back before he gets into any *more* trouble."

"Yes. Well, then there's that other problem," Uncle Ainsley mumbled and shook his head. "We can't send him back without the time propulsion synchronizer."

"The time propulsion synchronizer?" I repeated.

"Correct," Uncle Ainsley said.

"What's that?"

"It's a device on the time machine that's located

just under the wooden rack. See?" I peeked in the time machine, and sure enough, there was a gaping hole the size of my fist in the wall with all the instruments. "Without it, I can't send Captain Billy back."

"Where is it?" I asked the logical question.

"Captain Billy stole it," my uncle explained. "Right after we got home from McDonald's. I don't know where he hid it."

"So until we find it, we can't send the captain back?" I asked.

"Correct," Uncle Ainsley said. "But I've looked everywhere. I can't think where it could be."

"Can't you just make another time propulsion syn — , syn —"

"Just call it the T.P.S.," Uncle Ainsley said, waving his hand wearily. "Yes, I could make another one —"

"Why don't you?" I asked. "Then all our problems would be solved."

"I would, but — well —" Uncle Ainsley's face got a little red. "I can't remember exactly how I made it. It was rather complicated."

"Didn't you write down your plans for the time machine?" I asked. "Maybe it'll be in your notes."

"Uncle Ainsley gazed at me with a blank look. "Notes?" he said. "Yes, that would've been a good idea."

I sighed. "Uncle Ainsley, when we find the
T.P.S. — *if* we ever find it —"

My uncle winced.

"— how *will* we get the pirate to go back home
to 1699? If he really doesn't *want* to go back, how
will we get him into the time machine? He looks
pretty strong. We wouldn't be able to force him."

"Well, we'll worry about that once we find the
T.P.S.," Uncle Ainsley said, shrugging. "And
don't ask me how we'll do that!"

"So what'll we do until then? We can't let the
pirate go around breaking into stores. What if he's
caught? Couldn't you be in big trouble?"

"Why, yes," Uncle Ainsley said. "I never
thought of that. He *is* staying with me. I couldn't
lie under oath and say I didn't know about the
robbery at Rick's Radio and TV. And knowing
about the robbery would make me an accessory
to the crime."

"You're harboring a criminal!" I said.

"Oh, my," Uncle Ainsley said, wincing and putting a hand to his head as if he'd just gotten a
headache.

"We've just got to keep an eye on him," I said.

"Well, that won't be easy," said Uncle Ainsley.
"Especially when I'm teaching my classes or when
you're in school."

"We'll just have to find entertaining things for

Captain Billy to do while we're busy," I suggested as we started up the basement steps. "Just to keep him out of trouble."

"That might work," Uncle Ainsley said, climbing the stairs right behind me.

We walked through the kitchen and into the living room. I stopped suddenly. "Say, Uncle Ainsley, do you hear anything?"

Uncle Ainsley tilted his head to one side. "No. Why?"

"Neither do I," I said. "Isn't Billy watching TV?"

"Uh-oh," Uncle Ainsley said, and we both ran down the hall.

Uncle Ainsley grabbed the doorknob and shoved the door open. I ran in behind him.

Uncle Ainsley clutched my arm, and I looked into his terrified eyes as he stammered, "C-Captain Billy's gone!"

4

Uncle Ainsley was right. Except for the chicken leg lying on the carpet near the TV, there was no sign of Captain Billy. The side window was open.

Uncle Ainsley rushed to the window and craned his neck to look up and down the street, then paced nervously over to where the captain had been sitting earlier. He kicked absentmindedly at the chicken bone with his toe. It stuck to the beige carpet.

"What do we do now?" I asked.

"I guess we'd better find him," Uncle Ainsley answered, looking bewildered and scared. "I've never been in jail before," he mumbled with a worried frown.

"Don't worry, Uncle Ainsley," I assured him. "We'll find him."

"I hope so, my boy," he said.

"Where should we start?" I asked.

"I think we'd better split up," my uncle answered. "We can cover more ground. You start with the south side of town, and I'll take the north."

"Right!" I said, starting down the hall. Then I stopped. "What kind of place would attract Captain Billy?" I asked Uncle Ainsley, who was right behind me.

"I'm afraid, T.J., that the places that would draw the captain's attention are the places with the most people. He loves crowds."

"Great," I said, rolling my eyes. "I can't wait to find him."

"We *must* find him!" Uncle Ainsley said. "I'm harboring a criminal!"

Uncle Ainsley dressed quickly, and minutes later I watched him drive off down the street. As I picked up my bike, I glanced up just in time to see Mrs. Harkle's nose and one eye peeking out between her front curtains. I smiled and waved, and the curtain snapped back into place.

I got a running start, threw a leg over the back of my bike, and took off down Maple Drive.

Crowds, I thought. Where are there crowds on Saturday morning? It was about time for the stores to open downtown, so I veered off to the left.

I rode up and down the streets of downtown Cedar Springs, keeping a sharp lookout for the pirate. It'd be pretty hard for a guy in that getup to disappear into a crowd.

I didn't see him. I also didn't see anyone who looked as if they'd just seen a pirate. By that I mean I didn't see anyone walking down the street looking either shocked or terrified.

I guess he didn't go downtown, I thought, as I doubled back.

I rode along Main Street, heading north, and scanned every side street I passed, hoping to see some activity that could have been caused by Captain Billy.

Nothing.

Just then I happened to notice the big red-and-yellow McDonald's sign ahead. I decided to stop. After all, Uncle Ainsley said that Billy loved Big Macs, so it was a reasonable place to look. And besides, I hadn't eaten yet that day and my stomach had been growling ever since I'd left Uncle Ainsley's.

I swerved into the parking lot and put my bike in the rack.

I was just about to pull open the heavy glass door when I saw a movement at the corner of my eye. I turned just in time to see Captain Billy, in all his pirate finery, striding across the parking lot, heading right for me!

I quickly slipped inside and ducked behind a

large green plant to the right of the entrance. Billy strode up to the door and pulled it open. He stopped just inside, removed his tall feathered hat, and tucked it under one arm. He looked around uncertainly.

The girl behind the counter stared, motionless, at the pirate standing in front of her, her eyes wide. She looked like she was about seventeen, and wore her blonde hair pulled back in a ponytail.

"Can I help you?" she finally asked.

Another McDonald's worker, a boy about her age, had also noticed Billy and stopped suddenly in his route from the french fryer to the counter. He stared at the pirate from over the girl's shoulder.

Billy looked around as some of the patrons at tables off to the side of the restaurant stopped their chewing and conversations to gape at him.

"Uh, yeah," Captain Billy finally said to the girl behind the counter. "Gimme one of those . . . those —" He looked around, then up at the food under the hot lights.

"He wants a Big Mac," I blurted out from my place behind the plant. I slapped a hand over my big mouth, but it was too late.

Billy turned to look at me inquisitively as I left my hiding place and took a step toward him. Then he turned back to the girl and said, "Right! A Big Mac!"

The girl scurried back to get his burger and Billy turned toward me again. I tried to smile at him but it was a real effort, since I was so scared.

Then I hurried past him up to the counter and said, "Make that two Big Macs and two Cokes."

The girl slid the burgers across the counter to me and then filled the drink cups. I paid for the order and carried the food over to the seating area. I made my way to a back corner table behind another large plant, a potted tree, all the while knowing there were dozens of eyes on me. But the one I feared most was Captain Billy's.

Billy followed me at a distance, and when I reached the table and glanced back at him, he was scrutinizing me carefully from about fifteen feet away.

I sat down and picked up my Big Mac in trembling hands. "Hungry?" I asked and forced myself to take a bite.

The captain slowly approached and sat in the chair opposite me. He picked up his burger and pushed nearly a third of it into his mouth.

While he chewed, he studied me with a narrowed eye. Then, around the chewed up Big Mac, he said, "Yer the lad from the alley last night.

How come you showed at Weed's this mornin'? Come to arrest me?" His eye sparkled with this last question. I suppose he thought that was very funny.

"No, Captain Billy," I said. It occurred to me then that I had no idea how I would get him back to Uncle Ainsley's house. Maybe I should make friends with him, I thought. "I've never met a pirate before," I said. "Is it fun living on the sea?"

"Fun?" the pirate grunted. "It's a livin'." He grabbed his Coke and gulped some of it down. He suddenly pulled the cup away from his mouth, surprised. "What's this here?"

"Oh, yeah, you've never had Coke before," I said.

"Coke?" He sniffed the edge of the glass. "It sparkles in me mouth." He tried a sip and then another. "And sweet," he said. Then he downed the rest of it. He belched loudly and, slapping the cup down in front of him, wiped his mouth on the dirty lace that was hanging out of his sleeve.

"So why are ye here, laddie?" he asked, studying me with his large dark eye.

"Well, Captain Billy, you see, my Uncle Ainsley is pretty worried about you."

"Ainsley?" he asked suspiciously.

"Ainsley Weed, the guy who brought you here."

"Weed's yer uncle?" Billy asked. "Why's he worried about me?"

"Well, you see, he's . . . well, he's sort of responsible for you." Billy raised one eyebrow. I hurried on. "And, you see, if anybody finds out that you were the one who ripped off Rick's Radio and TV, then my uncle could get thrown in jail along with you. Because he knows about the burglary and he's not going to turn you in."

"He's not?" the pirate asked.

"No."

"And why might that be?"

"Well, no one knows about his time machine. And he doesn't want to tell anyone. So you've got to stop breaking into stores, Captain Billy. You don't need to steal from anybody around here. Besides, you said stealing was 'just a living.' "

"Pirate life's profitable," he said, his eye glazing over with the memory. "Especially when I git hold of a ship loaded with gold or jewels . . . or find a treasure."

"Treasure?" I asked. "Have you found treasure?"

Billy regarded me suspiciously again. "Not yit," he said.

"Then you're looking for treasure?" I asked.

Billy's left eye met mine. (I couldn't see the

right eye. It was under the patch.) "I'd say that's *my* business, matey," he replied.

"I suppose you miss it, though, don't you?" I asked.

"Miss it?"

"The pirate life. On your ship. You must be kind of homesick," I said.

"Naw," he grumbled. "I'm stayin' here."

"Did you ever meet any famous pirates?" I asked. "Like Captain Kidd?"

In one quick movement, he reached over the table and grabbed my shirt at the collar, hauling me halfway over the top of the table.

"What d'ye know about Cap'n Kidd?" he growled.

Something told me I'd asked the wrong question. "N-Nothing," I said. "I've just heard of him, that's all."

"And how would that be?" he asked.

"From one of my uncle's books," I said. He still held on to me. "Could you please let go of my shirt, Captain Billy?"

Billy seemed to consider my request for a moment, then slowly released his hold. I let out a long breath and sank back in my chair.

"Thanks," I said.

Captain Billy shoved his empty Coke glass in

my direction. "Gimme another Coke drink, lad," he said.

I lost no time getting up to the counter and ordering what he wanted. It took all the money I had left in my pocket. I sure hoped he wouldn't want anything more. The girl behind the counter watched me suspiciously as she slid the Coke over to me.

She leaned halfway over the counter and said in a whisper, "Who *is* that guy?" She pointed in Billy's direction.

I took a big breath. "Oh. Uh, he's a friend of mine," I said, while I racked my brain for a good story to explain who Billy was.

The girl looked at me uncertainly.

"He's . . . he's an actor!" I said. "He's just practicing his role." I studied the girl's face for any sign that she might've bought it.

The girl nodded, apparently satisfied. I grabbed the Coke and hurried back to our table.

Only Billy wasn't there. The table was empty.

"Well, T.J. O'Brien! My first day of spring vacation from Lincoln Junior High, and I have to run into *you*! Yuck! Some vacation!" Hearing that nasty voice, I knew immediately who was talking. I turned around to see Elizabeth Whitmore walking past me with one hand on her hip, the other cradling a McDonald's tray piled with burgers and Cokes.

Elizabeth is the most obnoxious kid in the sixth grade. Ask anyone. Her father is the chief of police in Cedar Springs, and she thinks that's a very big deal. As if everyone should bow down to *her* because her father is head of the police department.

The first time I ever saw Elizabeth she was scaring some little second-graders, telling them she was going to have her father arrest them because they had ridden their bikes on the sidewalk. The little girls believed her and tearfully begged Elizabeth not to tell. All the while, Elizabeth stood over them and laughed. I couldn't stand it, so I walked over and told the kids that Elizabeth was just a big bully, and not to worry, they weren't going to be thrown in jail. Elizabeth was furious.

And that's kind of the way it's been between Elizabeth and me ever since.

Just then I heard a squeal from behind me. I whirled around to see Captain Billy standing stiffly next to the water fountain. With one hand he pressed the button turning on the water. With the other hand he covered the fountain hole where the water comes out, just enough so that the water squirted high into the air and splashed all over the walls on the other side of the restaurant and dripped down on the tables and plants and on anyone who happened to be in the way.

Elizabeth Whitmore just happened to be one of the people in the way. She started screaming as the cold water showered over her. Grabbing her tray she ran to a dry spot across the room, but not before getting drenched by the frigid water.

Other kids seemed to enjoy it. They, of course, were the dry ones, the lucky people who'd sat down on the other side of the restaurant. They laughed and hollered and pushed each other closer to the waterfall. A young mother grabbed her little girl and ran out the door.

"Who *is* this guy?" a high school boy yelled.

"What a weirdo," someone said, and all of the kids (except for Elizabeth Whitmore) laughed and squealed and watched Billy with amazed expressions.

And all the while, Captain Billy stood entranced next to this water machine he'd just discovered, mumbling, "Well, blow me down. Blow me down."

Just then the McDonald's manager came around the corner to find out what all the commotion was about. When he saw Billy and the kids and the water dripping all over everything, he froze on the spot.

"Look what that maniac did!" Elizabeth screamed at him.

If I hadn't been so scared, I would have laughed. Elizabeth's hair was soaked and matted to her head. Her sweatshirt clung to her back and sagged at the bottom. She looked like a drowned rat.

But I didn't have time to enjoy the scene. I had to get Captain Billy out of there.

I dropped my Coke on the nearest table, ran to Billy and, grabbing him by the arm, dragged him out a side door.

"Let's go somewhere else, Captain," I said, pushing him from behind. He started across the parking lot, and I ran to the rack to grab my bike. I glanced back at the restaurant window to see about fifteen people, some of them with their noses squished against the glass, watching us.

And to the side of the group stood Elizabeth Whitmore, her face red with anger. She ran to the door and pushed it open.

"Just wait till my dad hears about this, O'Brien!" she yelled. "You and that pirate guy are in a lot of trouble!"

5

That was when it hit me, when Elizabeth Whitmore said she'd get us in trouble.

Her father was the chief of police!

If she really *did* tell her father about Billy — and if you knew Elizabeth Whitmore the way *I* do, you'd know it'd be stupid to bet against it — would the police come after Billy? And then Uncle Ainsley?

Now that Elizabeth knew about the pirate, it was *really* important to keep him out of sight. If only we could send him back to 1699!

I caught up with Captain Billy halfway down the block. He was moving at a pretty fast clip for a guy his size.

"Where're you going, Captain?" I asked. I was pedaling hard just to keep up with him.

He kept on walking and didn't answer.

"Captain Billy?" I was beginning to breathe hard as I rode along next to him. I didn't know how I'd ever get him back to my uncle's house.

"Captain Billy? Mind if I come along?"

Still no answer.

Suddenly he took off running across the street and into a wooded area. If he headed in a straight line, he'd come out of the woods near the lake on the edge of Jolly Dan's Amusement Park. But if he veered off in either direction, I was sure I'd lose him among the trees, which covered a half-mile stretch in either direction. I watched him in his crimson coat bobbing up and down as he ran off into the distance, getting farther and farther away.

It was hard following him on my bike. There were no trails, and the ground was bumpy and filled with weeds and wildflowers. Just as I thought I was about to lose sight of him, I spotted him heading toward the fence at the edge of the park.

Jolly Dan's Amusement Park was just opening its season that Saturday morning. People were already sailing on the lake in Jolly Dan's rented boats. The rides had been set up earlier in the week. I could see people in bucketlike seats riding up and over on the big Ferris wheel. And I could hear the excited screams of kids on the roller coaster. The rides towered over the multicolored game and snack booths inside the park.

Captain Billy stopped abruptly at the fence, grabbed hold of the chain links, slid the toe of his boot into an opening in the mesh, and climbed to the top. He hoisted himself over with a grunt, leaped off the top, and landed with a dull thud on the other side, while the metal fence *thwanged* against a nearby post.

"Captain Billy!" I called. "You can't just climb the fence. That's illeg —"

I stopped myself mid-sentence. What am I saying? What does a pirate care about breaking the law? That's how he makes his living!

I studied the fence a minute and then checked around to see if anyone was watching. All clear. So I climbed the fence just as Billy had done a few seconds before.

Then I realized it. I had broken the law, too. Uncle Ainsley might be *harboring* a criminal, but I had *become* one. For a fleeting moment, I wondered if there would be room for me, too, in Uncle Ainsley's cramped prison cell.

I didn't have time to think about it very long, though, because I had to catch up with Billy. If I could just keep him from getting caught breaking the law, Uncle Ainsley and I wouldn't have to go to jail. Even Elizabeth Whitmore's dad needs a *reason* to arrest someone.

Although it was still pretty early, Jolly Dan's was getting crowded. Young mothers and fathers were pushing strollers through the park and hanging on to little kids who were clutching cotton candy and blue-and-green Jolly Dan's balloons.

A crew from a local TV station was setting up, I guess, to tape a segment about the park's opening for the season. Terrific, I thought. Just what I need — Captain Billy running around and TV cameras all over the place.

I made my way through the crowd looking everywhere for him. There was an especially large group of people getting in line for the Ferris wheel.

That's where I spotted him. He was pushing his way through the throng, mumbling, "Pardon me, matey. Pardon me, lass."

Faster than you could blink an eye, as skilled as a master magician, his fingers slipped into a woman's open bag, slid out a wallet, and tucked it into his waistcoat. Captain Billy was *pickpocketing!*

Panic grabbed at my throat. I tried to call to Billy, but no words would come out.

Incredibly, no one saw what I saw. I say incredibly, because everyone was looking right at him, pointing him out to their children.

"See the pirate, honey? Oh, what fun!"

"I don't remember Jolly Dan's having a pirate last year!"

"Come on Shelly, come have your picture taken with the nice pirate!"

Billy just kept walking. He came my way, then seeing me, set off in the opposite direction.

I followed as best I could. He rounded the side of a snack booth and then suddenly stopped. I could see him from behind, his back straight and rigid, as he looked at something in front of him.

As I came around the side of the booth, I saw what he was staring at.

Two boys and a girl eating cotton candy stood in front of him. One boy had blue-dyed hair that stood straight up in a pointy ridge running from the front of his head to the back. He wore a baggy pink jacket over his T-shirt, designer jeans, and green Day-Glo sneakers. The other guy's hair was snow white, sticking straight up all over, and sprinkled with glitter. He wore a long red robe, and had shoes painted on his bare feet. The girl was perfectly bald; on her head, in place of hair, a paisley design was painted. She wore a black leotard, tights, and red shiny boots.

Billy stood there motionless, staring at the three kids, who still hadn't noticed him. I approached him from behind. He didn't seem to know I was there.

"Hi, Captain Billy," I said.

Billy didn't answer. He just kept staring with his mouth hanging open.

"Captain?" I said.

"Blimey," he said, not taking his eye off the group. "Blimey."

Just then the girl turned around and saw Billy and giggled, pointing at him. The boys turned, too, and looked him up and down. They laughed at him, and they all walked off, whispering about *his* costume.

"Captain Billy?" I said softly.

Billy watched them go. "Was that three lasses or two lads and a lass?" he wanted to know.

"Two lads and a lass," I said.

Slowly he turned to look at me. "Why were they —?" He stopped. "Never mind," he said. "I'm not sure I wants to know."

And with that, he stalked off.

"Captain Billy!" I said when I caught up with him.

"Why would it be that ye keep followin' me?" he asked irritably, not slowing down a bit.

"Like I said, Captain, I don't want you to get into trouble. Just take, for instance, that little pickpocketing episode back there."

Billy stopped suddenly and clapped a huge hand over my mouth. "That's dangerous talk, boy!" he growled at me. "Someone might hear ye. And ye don't want yer uncle to be sent to prison, do ye now, boy?"

I shook my head no, and he released me with a sly smile. "Don't worry, lad, I never get caught." He resumed walking.

Right, I thought. At least not yet.

"But, Billy, wait!" I said.

He rounded another snack booth near the front entrance to the park and stopped short.

"What's wrong?" I asked.

I followed his gaze. We were standing before a man-made pond just inside the park entrance. In front of the pond was a sign that read, JOLLY DAN WELCOMES YOU!

Next to the sign was a giant plastic statue of Jolly Dan, "The Happy Pirate." Interestingly, he looked a lot like Captain Billy. I hadn't noticed the resemblance till that moment.

But Billy wasn't looking at his plastic look-alike. His eye was fixed on what was sitting out in the middle of the pond.

A replica of a seventeenth-century pirate ship.

"Oh, yeah," I said. "That ship's been here since I was a little kid."

"Blow me down," Billy whispered to himself.

I stood there beside him and gazed over at the ship. Next to it was a sign with big black-and-gold letters reading "The *Brigantine* — From the Golden Age of Piracy! Board at your own risk!"

The ship is smaller than a real pirate ship would be. I think a real ship would take up the whole pond, and then some. The ducks who take up residence there in the summer would hate that.

The *Brigantine* held two small masts that towered over her. The large, square canvas sails fluttered in the breeze, along with a flag bearing a black-and-white skull and crossbones. They made a "thwapping" sound overhead. At the top of the mainmast was a little crow's nest.

If you board the ship, you can explore the miniature upper deck, examine the heavy rope riggings, or play on the two phony cannons.

It's really kind of a neat ship, but I hadn't really *looked* at it in years. Now Captain Billy was staring at it as if he'd come home.

"Is it like your ship, Captain Billy?" I asked him.

"Aye, 'tis," he answered softly, without taking his eye off the ship. "Small, but the spittin' image o' me ship, the *Midnight Revenge*."

"Did you like sailing?" I asked.

"There's nothin' like it," he said, his voice soft and far away. "The feel o' the salty wind in yer face, the smell o' the sea before a rain. Nothin' like it."

"You miss it?" I asked.

"Aye," he said.

"Gee, Captain Billy, if you're so homesick —"

"Homesick!" Suddenly Captain Billy snapped back to life. "What, me, homesick? Not on your life, boy!" Billy straightened up and spat on the ground. "Ye won't catch Cap'n Billy moonin' around like some sick little pup!"

"But you can have all that again!" I said, gesturing to the ship sitting in the pond. "The salty wind, the smell of the sea before a rain —"

But Captain Billy wasn't listening. He had turned and shoved his way through the small crowd of curious people who'd begun to gather while we'd been standing there.

I watched him disappear once again into the crowd.

By now, the park was really mobbed. Jolly Dan's is sort of "the place to go" in Cedar Springs on its opening day, and Billy didn't have any trouble losing me once the crowd had moved in.

I looked all over the park for the next two hours. I even asked a few people if they'd seen the guy dressed up as "Jolly Dan," saying that he was my father, and I had to find him to tell him my sister was sick. The story got better the more I told it. At the end of the two hours, my sister Belle had fallen from her prize horse while she was riding to warn a family that their house was on fire. She had broken her leg and was lying unconscious in the hospital that very minute, a heroine.

During the last half hour, no one reported having seen a pirate, but many people wished little Belle their best. That sort of made me feel guilty. I don't even have a sister. Anyway, I figured Captain Billy was long gone.

I really felt terrible. I'd let Uncle Ainsley down. What was I going to tell him? That darned pirate was just too tricky. Even if I found him again, how would I have gotten him to come home with me?

I'd tried being honest with him, explaining how much trouble my uncle would be in if Billy were caught doing something illegal. That sure didn't work. Less than a half hour later, he was pickpocketing.

And I had to go home and tell Uncle Ainsley that Billy was still on the loose somewhere. Probably getting into some awful trouble. By that time

Chief of Police Whitmore would probably know all about him.

I could just about hear those prison doors clang shut.

I pulled my bike out of the bushes and headed toward home.

6

"TV dinners again?" my dad said. He was standing in the kitchen doorway watching my mom pull out the frost-covered boxes from the freezer. He'd obviously just walked home from the college. His tie was loosened at the neck, he was carrying his sport coat, and his hair was windblown and messy. He was holding the evening paper.

"Hi, hon," my mom said and kissed him. "I know it's my turn to cook, but I was held up at school. Two kids were late for opera rehearsal, so that set everything back."

Mom had changed into her jeans and a T-shirt as soon as she'd come home from school. ("Getting normal" is what she calls it.) She teaches voice at the college's music department.

"What is it about music students?" Dad asked. "Business majors are much more reliable."

"And considerably less interesting," my mom

said, watching Dad out the corner of her eye.

Like a pro, she fielded the newspaper he threw at her. "Thanks," she said, catching it and giving him a crafty look as she unfolded it. "I wanted to see the headlines."

"You set me up!" my dad said, looking exasperated, and not a little impressed.

My Hungry Man Dinner tasted pretty good, especially since I hadn't eaten since breakfast at McDonald's. (But I don't think that day's meals were what my health teacher, Ms. Ling, had in mind when she lectured us about nutritional eating habits.)

"Mind if I switch on the news?" Dad asked after he'd taken a bite of fried chicken off his aluminum plate.

"To take your mind off your dinner?" Mom asked.

"Exactly," he answered.

"Oh, I don't know," she said. "I kind of like frozen instant whipped potatoes."

"Especially on the nights you cook," Dad observed with a smile as he flipped on the TV set that sits next to our breakfast nook table.

The six o'clock news was about half over. As the picture warmed up, one of the anchors finished a story about a local fire. Channel 6 has two anchors: a man and a woman; my mom calls them "Barbie and Ken" because she says they're so cute they look like plastic dolls instead of real people.

The picture came into focus, and "Ken," a chisel-chinned blond guy, smiled into the camera and said, "And next, a story about the opening of Jolly Dan's Amusement Park. Something new has been added this year: a real-live pirate! The strange thing is that Jolly Dan's manager claims to have no knowledge of this new employee. We'll meet the pirate and talk to the park manager after these messages."

I nearly choked on a mouthful of cherry cobbler. My parents looked at me, startled.

"T.J., are you all right?" my mom asked.

"Something go down the wrong way?" My dad thumped on my back.

I grabbed my glass of milk and washed down a mouthful of cherries. Whole.

I coughed. "I'm okay," I said.

That was true if you didn't count the fact that my heart was racing, my palms were sweating, and my stomach was suddenly where my Adam's apple was supposed to be.

The commercials were over and on came the news team again. "Ken" continued the reporting.

"It seems that Jolly Dan's Amusement Park has a new employee — that its management never hired. We have the story now from Jeff Smoke."

They cut to a videotape of the Ferris wheel at Jolly Dan's that afternoon. A voice came on. "This *was* to be a story about the opening of one of Cedar Springs's favorite entertainment spots, Jolly Dan's Amusement Park. It turned into quite another story."

The camera panned the crowd and stopped on a familiar-looking guy with a crimson waistcoat and a patch over his right eye. Guess who.

"We met a very interesting gentleman in the crowd at Jolly Dan's," the reporter said. "He said his name was Captain Billy. We logically assumed he was hired to play Jolly Dan and greet parkgoers on this opening day."

Jeff Smoke, the reporter, approached Captain Billy on the tape. "Good morning, you must be Jolly Dan," he said.

Captain Billy looked surprised for a moment and stared at the reporter. "Me name's Cap'n Billy," he said, sounding as confused as he looked.

"Well, it's good to meet you, Captain Billy," the reporter said, glancing with a smile at the camera. "How is business on your opening day?"

"Business?" Captain Billy glared at Jeff Smoke

63

suspiciously. "And what is yer meanin' about me business?"

The reporter laughed and shrugged. "Well, the pirating business, of course." He turned to grin at the camera. "Robbing ships, stealing treasure, that sort of thing."

Billy didn't answer, and I could see he was getting mad because his one visible eye narrowed to a little slit, and he drew himself up to his full, towering height.

The reporter was obviously flustered. "Did I say the wrong thing?" he joked, taking a step back. "Have you seen any of your buddies lately? Blackbeard, Captain Kidd —"

Captain Billy whipped out his sword so fast I hardly saw it happen. "Captain Kidd, eh?" he said, brandishing the sword in front of him, threatening the reporter.

"Good heavens!" my mother said, leaning toward the TV. "Is this report a put-on?"

"Shhhh!" I said.

"Uh, well, sorry to bother you, Captain Billy," the reporter said, backing away with his arms held up in front of himself, and forcing a laugh. "Looks like we caught you on a bad day."

The reporter took a few more hurried steps away from Billy, and his voice came over the tape and said, "After our encounter with this strange guy, we talked with Dan Whalen, the manager and owner of Jolly Dan's."

They cut to a picture of the owner, who turned beet red when the reporter described what had happened. "I have no such employee," the man said. "I'm calling the police. And if he comes around again, I'll have him arrested for assault!"

The reporter turned to face the camera again and said, "Well, there you have it, folks. A strange story, indeed. Mr. Whalen promises to call in the police department to investigate fully. We'll follow the story, and if there are any developments, we'll be sure to let you know. Jeff Smoke, Channel 6 Action News."

I was shaking all over, but trying to remain in control in front of my parents.

"That's the strangest thing I've ever seen in my life!" my mother said, and my father just shook his head in disbelief.

Just then the phone rang. "I'll get it!" I said, glad to get away before they noticed I was acting strangely.

I grabbed the phone before its second ring. "T.J.?" a voice whispered on the other end.

"Yes?" I said.

"Can you get over here right away?" I recognized Uncle Ainsley's voice.

"What happened? Did you see the news?" I asked.

"Just get over here!" he said.

"What happened?" I asked anxiously.

"Captain Billy!" he said. "He just walked in the door! Come quick! You have to help me keep him here!"

7

Within ten minutes, I'd parked my bike in front of Uncle Ainsley's house. He must have been watching for me because he yanked the door open before I had time to ring the bell.

"Well, come in, my boy, come in!" he said in a big loud welcome. "What a nice surprise!"

I figured he didn't want Billy to know he'd made the emergency call to my house. I wondered how he'd done it without Billy knowing. It hadn't been easy on my end, either. I'd made an excuse about Uncle Ainsley needing a guinea pig for one of his experiments, and I rushed out before my parents could argue.

Uncle Ainsley glanced back over his shoulder. Not seeing Billy there, my uncle pulled me into the living room and spoke in an urgent whisper.

"T.J., we've got to get rid of Captain Billy! I'm afraid the police will be closing in soon!"

Uncle Ainsley's eyes were filled with fear. I

put what I hoped was a steadying hand on his shoulder.

"I know," I whispered back. (I didn't tell him about seeing Elizabeth Whitmore at McDonald's. That would only have upset my uncle more.) "Uncle Ainsley, I don't see how we'll ever find the T.P.S. And even if we do, we can't *make* Captain Billy go back if he doesn't want to. We've got to find some way of persuading the captain he *wants* to go home to 1699. Now think — what's important to him? What would make Billy *want* to return home?"

"Well," my uncle said, rubbing his chin, "he's a pirate. He likes — well, stuff that pirates like."

"That's it!" I said. "*Treasure!* He likes treasure! If we could only come up with a treasure!"

"We don't have that kind of money, my boy," Uncle Ainsley said, shaking his head.

"No," I said, "I mean, maybe we could find a treasure from his own time — you know, the 1690s!"

Uncle Ainsley looked at me thoughtfully.

"Where's the grub ye promised me, Weed?"

We whirled around to see an angry-looking pirate standing in the living room doorway.

"I'm mighty hungry," he complained, rubbing his stomach.

"Now, Captain, I'll fix you some food right away," my uncle said. "Just sit down and talk with T.J. here while I fix some meat loaf for you."

Just then the doorbell rang.

Uncle Ainsley's mouth opened, but no sound came out. "What do we do?" he mouthed the words silently, his eyes imploring for me to give him a quick answer.

Captain Billy seemed to be studying the wall around the corner in the hall. "What was that sound, Weed? What was that ringin' sound?"

"Get the captain back in the den," I whispered.

The doorbell rang again.

"It's coming from this box," Billy mumbled to himself, staring up at the doorbell chimes near the ceiling. "It couldn't be a timepiece. It's not near the hour." He grabbed a chair nearby, dragged it over close to the bell, and climbed up to get a better look.

"Get him into the den!" I whispered again. Uncle Ainsley was frozen with fear.

Whoever was waiting on the porch got impatient then and started banging on the door.

"Someone's at your door, Weed," Billy said. He stepped off the chair and headed for the front door.

"No, no, I'll get it!" I yelled and grabbed the

captain by the arm. "You go and watch the television." I gestured wildly to my uncle. "Right, Uncle Ainsley? Why don't you find something for Billy to watch?"

My uncle snapped into action. "Oh, yes! Good idea! I have a great movie for you to see on my VCR! It's one called *Moby Dick!*" Uncle Ainsley said, clapping his hands and talking the way you do to a three-year-old. "It's about a *whale!*"

The banging started up again at the door.

"Are ye goin' te see who's at yer door, Weed?" Billy said impatiently, trying to push past me to answer it.

"Oh, don't worry about that," I said, pushing back. "I'll get the door and Uncle Ainsley will start the movie for you. Then before the movie's over, your dinner will be ready."

The mention of food did the trick. Billy stopped pushing, grunted, and sauntered into the den.

"Start the movie!" I whispered to my uncle. "I'll get the door."

"What if it's the police?" he said. "Did you see the news?"

"I don't know and yes," I said miserably. "Just go start the movie!"

The banging started at the door again just as Billy yelled, "Well, Weed, are ye comin' or not?"

"Right away!" my uncle said and scurried into

the den, closing the door behind him.

I hurried to the door and opened it.

Mrs. Harkle rushed in. "Oh, thank goodness you're all right!" Mrs. Harkle said. "You are, aren't you?" She peered into my face as if she might see something wrong if she studied it hard enough.

"Sure," I said, trying to calm my heart which was banging loudly in my chest.

"He's here, isn't he?" she cried.

"Who? What?" I said.

"I saw that pirate from tonight's news! I saw him walk in the front door a few minutes ago! I was really worried, and then I saw you arrive, and your uncle looked so scared when he opened the door!"

What was she doing? I wondered. Using a telescope? How could she have seen Uncle Ainsley's expression in the doorway from all the way across the street?

"Oh, no!" I said. "Everything's fine."

Just then Uncle Ainsley appeared from the hall.

"Everything's fine, isn't it, Uncle Ainsley?" I said. "There's no pirate here, is there?" I forced myself to laugh.

"A pirate?" my uncle said. "Oh, no. No pirate here."

"But I saw him come in!" she insisted. "He

looked just like the pirate on the news!"

"No," I said. "Oh, maybe you're thinking of my friend Marcus. He stopped by for a minute. He just left — by the back door, in fact."

"Was he wearing a red coat?" Mrs. Harkle asked.

"Yes, he was," I said. (Well, if I really *had* a friend named Marcus, I'm sure he'd wear a red coat.)

Mrs. Harkle looked doubtful, but she relaxed a little. "Oh," she said. "Well, I feel a little foolish. I could've sworn . . ."

"No problem, Mrs. Harkle," my uncle said. He looked at me and nodded toward the kitchen. "Well, if you'll excuse me, I have to fix dinner right away."

"Oh?" she said.

"Uh, yes," Uncle Ainsley said. "You see, I have a guest coming for dinner."

"A guest?" she asked.

"Yes," I said. "He's coming pretty soon, so we'd better get at it."

"What are you going to prepare for your dinner?" asked Mrs. Harkle.

"Uh, well, I was going to make a meat loaf," said Uncle Ainsley.

"A meat loaf?" Mrs. Harkle laughed merrily. "For a dinner guest? Oh, how just like a man!"

"What do you mean?" I asked. "My dad is a better cook than my mother."

"But *meat loaf?*" Her eyes suddenly lit up. "I know! Why don't you let *me* fix your dinner!"

Uncle Ainsley and I looked at each other in a panic.

"Oh, n-no, no," Uncle Ainsley said. "I wouldn't hear of it. T.J. here is going to help me. I don't need any more help!"

"Nonsense!" Mrs. Harkle said. "Let me fix something appropriate for your special dinner guest. How about a nice *coq au vin?* Or — I know! *Veal cordon bleu!*" She said those words with an accent. I think it was French. "I just happen to have some fresh veal in my refrigerator and all the necessary ingredients! You just wait right here! I'll be back straight away!"

As soon as she was out the door, I rushed to Uncle Ainsley. "She's going to fix us dinner! Here in the kitchen! With Captain Billy in the den!"

"It appears that way," my uncle said.

"Well, what do we do now?" I asked. "What if Captain Billy decides he's tired of watching *Moby Dick* and makes a grand entrance demanding his food? What will we do then?"

"I'll just have to sit with him in the den and make sure he stays there," he said.

"Uncle Ainsley," I said. "No offense, but you're

not likely to stop him if he wants to leave the den."

Uncle Ainsley smiled. "Well, brains are better than brawn. You watch. I'll just use my head." He pointed to his forehead.

That's what I'm afraid of, I thought, but of course I didn't say it. Don't get me wrong, I love my Uncle Ainsley, but as you may have noticed, he *is* a bit scatterbrained sometimes.

Mrs. Harkle was back in a flash, reeking of some kind of strong perfume. I noticed it the minute she rushed through the door. I wondered if she'd spilled it on her dress by accident.

"All ready!" she sang out, hurrying into the kitchen.

Uncle Ainsley immediately ran into the den to watch over Billy.

I sat nervously at the kitchen table, keeping an eye on both my watch and Mrs. Harkle, hoping she was a fast cook. I didn't know how long the captain would stay in the den.

"Can I help you, Mrs. Harkle?" I asked.

"Oh, no, no!" she answered. "Just relax! Dinner will be ready in two shakes of a lamb's tail."

I didn't have any idea how long that was, so I just sat there with my stomach churning. And it wasn't from hunger.

Suddenly, from down the hall, I heard the den door open and shut loudly, and lumbering footsteps tromp toward the kitchen.

Oh, no! This is it! I thought. In a second, Billy will be in here, and Mrs. Harkle will know that he really is the pirate that the police are looking for. She'll go bananas, Billy will be arrested, and Uncle Ainsley will be thrown in jail to rot for the rest of his life.

But nothing happened. I mean, the footsteps stopped in the middle of the hall. I heard the bathroom door slam shut and then silence.

Uncle Ainsley peeked around the corner into the kitchen. Mrs. Harkle didn't see him. She was too busy slicing Swiss cheese and humming to herself.

Uncle Ainsley silently mouthed the words, "He's in the bathroom."

I nodded nervously, my heart pounding hard.

His head disappeared. Moments later, I heard the toilet flush and the bathroom door open.

Then suddenly, a huge, off-key singing voice boomed out down the hallway, "Yo-ho-ho, and a bottle of rum!"

Mrs. Harkle was so startled, she dropped the cheese slicer.

Luckily I thought fast. "I guess it's pretty surprising that Uncle Ainsley has such a big singing voice, don't you think?"

Mrs. Harkle looked confused. "Oh, my," she said. "His singing voice isn't anything like his speaking voice, is it? It's just so — well, so gruff, I guess you could say."

I heard some footsteps in the hallway. Uncle Ainsley must have guided the captain back to the den, because I heard the den door open and slam shut again.

I took a deep breath. That was close.

"Say, where *is* your uncle, anyway?" asked Mrs. Harkle, glancing at me out the corner of her eye as she crumbled up some crackers.

"Oh, I think he's busy in the den."

She smiled. "And when does your guest arrive?"

"Arrive?" I said. "Oh, well, any time now. Of course, you don't need to hang around and meet him. He's really a pretty boring guy, anyway." (Did I say *boring*?)

"Oh, but I'd love to meet any of your uncle's friends!" Mrs. Harkle exclaimed.

While I was thinking up an answer to that one, I heard the den door open again and feet stomp down the hall.

"How ken ye be makin' grub when yer watchin'

a movie with me?" boomed Billy's voice. "Where's me food?"

All at once, Billy's body loomed in the kitchen doorway. Mrs. Harkle, who was in the process of carrying her veal dish to the oven, looked up just in time to see the pirate's entrance.

The veal and cheese and ham and everything went splattering all over the kitchen floor.

And Mrs. Harkle just stood there staring, her mouth wide open.

8

It seemed that Mrs. Harkle couldn't move. She stood there staring at Billy, frozen in the middle of the kitchen floor with all the veal mess and shattered pieces of casserole dish around her feet. Some of the stuff had slopped up on her legs and the bottom edge of her dress, and her feet were practically buried in the stuff. Mrs. Harkle sure had made a lot of food.

Captain Billy pointed at the goo on the floor. "Is that me food?" he asked seriously.

I was afraid that if I said yes, he'd go over and start eating it off the floor or something.

"Uh, no, that isn't your dinner," I said.

"Then where is it?" asked the pirate. "And who's the lady?" He pointed directly at Mrs. Harkle.

"Oh, excuse me for not introducing you," Uncle Ainsley said, so nervous he was shaking. "Uh, Mrs. Harkle, this is . . . is —"

"Captain Billy," Billy said, prompting my uncle.

"Yes," my uncle said. "And Captain, this is Mrs. Harkle from across the street."

"Ma'am," Billy nodded politely to Mrs. Harkle. Uncle Ainsley turned to me with amazement written all over his face. Billy had *manners*!

Mrs. Harkle, all this time, hadn't moved a muscle, staring at Billy. Now she turned to my uncle.

"So there *was* a pirate here," she said. "The one I saw on the news tonight."

Uncle Ainsley and I looked at each other, not knowing what to say.

"Well, uh, yes, he was on the news," my uncle said.

A small note of alarm crept into Mrs. Harkle's voice. "And the police are looking for him?"

"The police?" asked Billy. Did I see a glint of fear in his eyes?

"Yes," Mrs. Harkle said. "They said on the news that the police are looking for you."

"Oh, that. Well, that was just — just a joke," I said. Billy was watching me closely.

"It was?" she said.

"Yes, you see, well, Billy's not a real pirate." I glanced at Billy to get his reaction. He didn't seem to mind. The mention of police really seemed to have shaken him up.

Mrs. Harkle, still standing there with food all

around her ankles, glanced over at Billy and back at me.

"What happened on the news was just part of an act," I said.

"What act?" Mrs. Harkle looked confused.

"Well, you see, he's Uncle Ainsley's friend," I said. "He's an expert on pirates."

"Another professor?" she asked.

"Uh, yes, right," I said, an idea forming in my mind. "He's a professor. A visiting professor. He's going to give a lecture at the college about pirate life."

"Ohhhh," Mrs. Harkle said, beginning to smile. "How nice." She nodded at the captain.

"And he calls himself Captain Billy, and he gives his lectures in full costume," I explained, beginning to enjoy my story. "Uncle Ainsley and I even call him Captain Billy when he's preparing his lectures to help him get into character." (Boy, I was really on a roll now.)

"Oh, how thrilling!" exclaimed Mrs. Harkle. "I do so wish I could hear his lecture. It must be fascinating!"

"Oh, you bet it is," I said, nodding and smiling at the captain, who looked more relaxed than he had a minute ago. "We're very proud of him."

Captain Billy stepped forward. "Sorry t'have startled ye, ma'am," he said.

Mrs. Harkle blushed a little and looked at the floor. It was only then, I guess, that it dawned on her that she was covered with food.

"Oh, goodness!" she said. "Just look at me; I'm a sight! And your lovely dinner is ruined!"

"No problem, Mrs. Harkle," I said. "We can just order a pizza or something."

"Oh, well, I'd better go and get cleaned up," she said. "I'm just thrilled to meet you, uh, Captain," Mrs. Harkle smiled at the captain and then at Uncle Ainsley, and she hurried through the living room and out the door.

"Man, was that close!" I said.

"Good thinking, my boy," Uncle Ainsley said, clapping me on the shoulder.

"So what about the police?" Billy asked.

"This is getting very serious, Captain Billy," I said. "The police *are* looking for you. We were able to convince Mrs. Harkle it was just part of an act, but the police won't fall for that. They'll check out your story, and when they find out what you've been up to, you'll be in big trouble . . . and so will we."

"I never get caught," he said, some of the old swagger returning. I rolled my eyes at Uncle Ainsley.

"So where's me food?" Billy asked.

* * *

81

After the pizza arrived and we'd had our fill (Billy ate more than half of it by himself — I wasn't all that hungry since I'd eaten at home), we settled down in Uncle Ainsley's living room, the captain in the brown recliner and Uncle Ainsley and me at opposite ends of the couch.

Captain Billy surprised us yet again. He was really calm and relaxed, just like a normal human being. He even told my uncle and me some adventure stories from the high seas and some raunchy pirate jokes that I won't repeat here.

After awhile, Billy looked over at me. "Ye know, ye haven't yet told me yer name, boy."

"Really?" I was surprised. "T.J."

"And what do the letters stand fer?" he asked.

"Timothy Joseph," I said.

"Timmy Joe," Uncle Ainsley said, smiling. "I used to call you Timmy Joe."

"Timothy Joseph," I repeated emphatically. Nobody calls me Timmy Joe anymore. Not if I can help it, anyway.

Just then, there was a frantic knock at the door.

Uncle Ainsley, Billy, and I glanced at each other fearfully. My uncle turned on the front porch light and peeked out the little window in the door. Billy got himself ready to run if it became necessary.

"Why, it's Mrs. Harkle," Uncle Ainsley said.

He opened the door a crack, and she pushed it open and flounced into the room with a big smile. "Ainsley, T.J., Professor-Captain, I have the most wonderful news!" she said. "I've just been on the phone with the head of the Ladies' Historical Society, an organization of which I am a member. Anyway, the guest speaker at tomorrow's luncheon became ill at the last minute and cannot come to our meeting. Soooo," she hesitated, very pleased with herself, "so I suggested that I just *might* know of someone who could come in at the last minute to lecture on the topic of pirate life on the high seas! None other than our friend, Captain Billy!"

She stopped talking, waiting, I guess, for us to cheer.

We didn't.

Mrs. Harkle looked surprised at our lack of enthusiasm. "Well, of course, the club will provide remuneration!"

I'd never seen Uncle Ainsley look so scared.

"Oh, thank you," I stammered, "but, Mrs. Harkle, Billy's pretty busy here, and I don't think —"

"Ma'am?" The captain stood up and faced Mrs. Harkle. "Is it me understandin' that ye're invitin' me te talk about me life at sea?"

"Yes, and you'll be our guest. Lunch at the Golden Palate Restaurant!" Mrs. Harkle had decided to sweeten the pot.

"Oh, Billy," I said, noticing that my uncle's face had turned a dull shade of gray, "don't feel obliged to speak to the Ladies' Historical Society. You have a *lot* of other things to do." Oh please, oh please, don't say you'll go to the meeting, I pleaded silently. (How could he even consider it? A minute ago, he was scared to death the cops were coming for him.)

"Well, blow me down, ma'am, I'd be mighty pleased te talk te the ladies. They'll hear some great sea stories — from the greatest captain of 'em all!"

"What an actor!" Mrs. Harkle gushed.

Uncle Ainsley and I just stood there, speechless and horrified.

9

T. J., what on earth is going on?" Mom demanded the minute I walked in the door. She and Dad had obviously been pacing the living room for some time, awaiting my arrival.

"What do you mean?" I asked.

"The police were here!" Dad said. "Not half an hour ago!"

"Inquiring about that pirate on the news!" Mom said. "The officer said someone reported that you knew the man! Something about a — a water-squirting incident at McDonald's —"

Obviously the work of Elizabeth Whitmore. *The rat!*

"They must have wanted a different T.J. O'Brien," I said. "How would I know a pirate?"

My mother looked serious. "T.J., does this have anything to do with my brother? You've been spending an awful lot of time with Ainsley the past couple days, and he can really get himself into —"

"Mom!" I forced out a small laugh. "Uncle Ainsley? Come on! How could either of us possibly know that guy on the news? Uncle Ainsley has been working day and night on his new invention. And I've been helping."

Technically, I was sort of telling the truth.

Then I realized something. It wasn't safe at home anymore. The police would surely be back again to question me. I had to get out of there before they came back!

"Uh, Mom, Dad, I just came home to grab my toothbrush and a change of clothes —"

"Oh, no, T.J., we need to talk about this —" my dad began.

"*Please*, Dad, Mom, it's critical to Uncle Ainsley's experiment! I have to stay with him. I told him I would. Just a day or two more. Then I'll be home more, I promise." They just had to let me go!

I directed my last appeal mostly to my mother, since she's more of a pushover than my dad. She likes to see me happy.

I could tell it was working. She was beginning to look concerned for me and my anxiety over disappointing my uncle.

I pressed on. "I can't let him down, Mom. You know how important his experiments are to him!"

Mom sighed. "All right, T.J."

"Wait a minute, Laura," my dad said. "Don't you think we'd better get to the bottom of this — ?"

"Tomorrow," Mom said gently. "T.J., tomorrow when you get home from Ainsely's, we'll all sit down and have a good, long talk."

"Laura —" my dad began.

"Honey, it's spring vacation," Mom said to him. "Just for tonight, let's let T.J. go."

Dad sighed. "Okay." Then he pointed a finger at my nose. "But tomorrow, young man, you've got some explaining to do."

"Thanks, Mom, Dad!" I said and shot Mom a grateful smile.

I rushed up to my room, grabbed some overnight stuff, and raced back over to Uncle Ainsley's house.

Even at my uncle's house, I didn't sleep well. I kept having nightmares about all of the terrible things that could go wrong at the luncheon the next day.

Uncle Ainsley said that maybe we could convince all the women, like we did Mrs. Harkle, that when Captain Billy threatened the reporter with his sword he was only acting.

But what if somebody checked out his story and

discovered he wasn't really a professor?

I was in the middle of one of those nightmares I told you about when I felt someone shaking my shoulder. At first, still in my dream, I thought the cops were dragging me off to jail, and I was fighting to get away.

I think I must have really taken a swing at one of the police officers, because when I opened my eyes, Captain Billy was standing over me with a big grin on his face.

"So yer a feisty lad after all," he said, chuckling. "Ye must've clobbered 'im plenty."

The sun slanted in the living room window and across the hardwood floor of my uncle's living room. The smell of bacon and eggs filled the air. My stomach growled.

The captain stood there a moment, towering over me, with his hands on his hips. Then he grinned again.

"Well, Timothy Joseph," he said in a surprisingly soft voice, "Me thinks yer awake now." He ruffled my already tousled hair. "Come on," he said. "Yer uncle and me was havin' some breakfast."

I got up and followed him into the kitchen where Uncle Ainsley was sitting at the table. I don't think he had gotten much sleep, either.

He looked terrible. I really felt sorry for him.

"Good morning, T.J., my boy," he said.

The captain sat back down and went after the rest of his food. It appeared to be eggs, sausages, and toast, but it was pretty gross-looking. All of it was piled in one messy heap in the middle of the plate, with yellow egg yolk running all over the place.

I decided to look out the window.

"Uncle Ainsley, are you going to the lecture with Captain Billy today?"

"Yes," he said, his head bent sadly over his eggs. "And that's not all. Mrs. Harkle called early this morning. She said that in an unprecedented move, the Men's Lodge, after hearing about Billy's lecture, asked to be included in today's meeting."

"The Men's Lodge?" I asked, incredulous. "They're going to join the women today? They *never* meet with outsiders!"

"Well, they are today," Uncle Ainsley said. "They're very anxious to hear our speaker." He glanced at Billy and rolled his eyes miserably.

"Captain, are you sure you want to go?" I asked him. "It could be very dangerous!"

"Aw, we fooled the lady last night," he said, sounding very confident. "And the ladies always love Cap'n Billy. I jest turn on me charm." He pushed back his empty plate and smiled, and there was egg yolk all over his teeth.

"You know, Captain Billy, that these people are kind of hard to please," I said. "They're really into manners and stuff."

"That'll be no problem," he said, leaning back in his chair and putting his boots up on the table. Then he began to pick his teeth with a knife.

"I think I'll go sit outside in the fresh air," I said. "Come out when you're done."

I sat on a lawn chair on the patio, and in a few minutes both Billy and my uncle joined me.

"Captain," I said. "Won't you tell us where the T.P.S. is? We might have to send you back in a hurry. You don't want to spend your life here if you have to be in prison."

"It's in a safe place," the captain said. "I found a good place last night."

"You were out by yourself last night?" Uncle Ainsley said, horrified. "With the police looking for you?"

"I move about all right in the dark," he said. "I'm quick on me feet."

"Captain Billy, I've been wondering, what were you doing the minute Uncle Ainsley's time machine grabbed you?" I asked.

90

"I was in sword play," he said.

"Sword play? You mean, you were fighting?"

"Aye," he answered.

"Who were you fighting?" I asked.

"Cap'n Kidd," he said. His eyes darkened at the memory.

"Captain Kidd?!" I couldn't believe it. Uncle Ainsley turned to the pirate, his eyes wide. "You were fighting the *real* Captain Kidd?"

"Aye."

"What were you fighting about?" I asked.

The captain sighed and gently patted his fist into his palm. "Treasure," he said.

"Wow!" I said. "Just like in the movies! There was a chest filled with gold and jewels, and you were trying to get it?"

"Aye," he said. "Kidd had just captured a Moorish ship, the *Quedah Merchant*. He had a chest full of silks, jewels, pieces of eight, and gold."

"I wonder what happened to the treasure," I said.

"I dunno," he said. "I wasn't there te find out." He shot my uncle an angry look.

Uncle Ainsley looked thoughtful, but he didn't say anything.

"Boy, just think what it'd be like to find all that treasure," I said.

91

"Aye," Billy said, a faraway look in his eye. Then he stood up abruptly. "Come on, boy," he said to me. "Let's be off."

My mouth dropped open. "Where? We can't go anywhere."

"Show me around town. I won't be sittin' still around this place," he said, pulling me up off the chair.

I could see I wasn't going to change his mind. "Then at least wear something different," I said. "You're too conspicuous in that get-up."

He agreed, and we all went to see what we could find in Uncle Ainsley's closet.

"These clothes will never fit him, Uncle Ainsley," I said. "Billy must be nearly a foot taller and sixty pounds heavier."

"Maybe my sweatsuit will work," my uncle said hopefully. "I got a large size just to wear around the house, to be comfortable."

He reached in the back of his closet and brought out a dark green sweatsuit. The captain took off his pirate clothes and pulled it on.

I had to bite the insides of my mouth to keep from laughing. The ankles of the pants were about six inches higher than they should've been. The sweatshirt, which zipped up the front, barely covered his middle. He kept tugging it down to cover his stomach. Uncle Ainsley's sneakers were much too small, so the pirate had to put his boots back on.

I took a quick shower and changed into fresh clothes.

Just as we were about to head out the back door (away from Mrs. Harkle's view), Uncle Ainsley pulled me aside.

"I'll meet you later at the Golden Palate," he said. "Keep Billy out of trouble."

"I'll try," I said. I followed Billy out the door.

I felt safer with Billy wearing the sweatsuit, even though he looked pretty ridiculous in it. No one recognized him, and we walked around a lot of Cedar Springs, including the college campus and downtown.

By late morning, we ended up at Jolly Dan's Amusement Park again. Today it wasn't opening until noon, so it was still locked up.

The gate didn't stop Captain Billy, though. He climbed over it just as he had the day before.

"Captain," I said, very nervous from outside the fence, "*please* don't do this to me. We can't go in there yet. *Please* come back out!"

"I want another look at the ship," he said. "Come on over, boy, we'll be out before anyone sees us."

"But —"

"The faster you git over here, the faster we leave," he said, a crafty look in his unpatched eye.

My heart thumping double time, I climbed over the fence, making myself a criminal twice in two days.

We hurried to the pond and stopped in front of the ship.

"I really don't think we should be here," I said uneasily, looking around for security guards.

"Keep yer britches on, son," Billy mumbled, not taking his eye off the ship. "I'm goin' te board her."

Slowly he stepped across the gravel path and up the small gangplank. He looked kind of funny, oddly out of place, his huge body walking the deck of this ship that was accurate in every detail, only kid-sized.

I followed close behind.

He strolled the deck, running his hand along the side of the ship, examining the wood. He gazed up into the sails that flapped in the breeze and took a big breath of air.

"Hey, you!"

Billy and I must've jumped about a foot in the air and whirled around to face two policemen at the end of the gangplank.

The mouth of the first cop dropped open when he got a good look at Captain Billy. He glanced at his partner beside him.

"It's the guy we've been looking for, the 'pirate' that pulled a knife on the TV reporter."

They both drew their guns and aimed them directly at us.

10

Just come down here quietly," the first cop said, beckoning with his hand. "You've just added breaking and entering to the charges that'll be filed against you."

"What are you going to do with us?" I asked him.

"I don't know yet about you, kid, but this pirate here has a lot of questions to answer."

While the officer and his partner led us toward their patrol car, one of them read us our rights. You know, you've heard it a million times on TV. Anything you say can and will be held against you in a court of law and all that stuff. But, believe me, it sounds different when the cop is reading it to *you*.

I felt sick to my stomach. In my whole life, the most trouble I'd ever been in was in the fourth grade when I was sent to the principal's office for fishing a tadpole out of the classroom aquarium and slipping it down Anita Ashford's dress. Now

I was being arrested and hearing my rights read. I'd really gone downhill since fourth grade. And there was no doubt in my mind that my parents would think the same thing.

And how in the world was I going to explain Captain Billy? Telling the truth would send Uncle Ainsley straight to jail.

All of these thoughts raced through my head as Billy and I trudged toward the car.

As I said, I felt miserable. But I didn't feel that way for long. That emotion was soon replaced by terror.

Because Billy suddenly whirled around to face the policeman with the pistol, kicked the weapon out of the guy's hand, and caught it — just like something you'd see on TV!

Then he raced to the patrol car, still holding the gun on the police officers and, as I watched him, horrified, he yanked out the wiring on their radio!

"Saw that trick on the TV," he bellowed to me proudly.

"Uh, I don't think this is a very good idea, Billy," I called to him, realizing that my voice was suddenly about an octave higher than usual. "We could get into a *whole* lot of trouble."

"You tell him, kid," said the cop who had just lost his gun.

"Haw, haw, haw," laughed Billy. "Now, gentlemen, if'n you'll be so kind as te step into your automobile." He gestured gallantly with the pistol and held open the door.

The two policemen got in, and Captain Billy waved me away some distance as he backed up toward me, still facing the patrol car. Then he pointed the pistol at the car.

"No, Billy! NO!" I screamed. "Don't shoot them! *Please don't!"*

The pistol fired. Twice.

"Don't worry, Timothy Joseph!" the pirate laughed, slapping me on the shoulder. "Just makin' sure they won't be followin' us!"

I looked to see both front tires drooping on the ground.

"Saw that on television, too," the captain said, grinning. "Come on, boy! No time to lose!"

He grabbed my arm and pulled me along. I don't know why I went along with him. I guess because I was terrified and didn't know what else to do.

Billy and I ran for a long time. We ran through backyards and alleys, not along the sidewalks or main roads. I was puffing hard, but not as hard as the captain, who was carrying around a lot of excess weight.

"Where're we going, Captain?" I asked.

Billy peered into the sky. "Lead me to the

Golden Palate, boy. The sun says it's time for me speech."

My jaw must've dropped nearly to my feet. "You're not still planning to talk to the Ladies' Historical Society and the Men's Lodge!" I said.

"I gave me word," he said simply.

I couldn't believe what I was hearing. "You mean, you've never gone back on your word?" I asked.

"All the time," Billy said and shrugged. "But me stomach needs feedin', and that dame said there'd be food."

"You just shot out the tires of a *police car!*" I screamed at him. "You'd be CRAZY to go to the meeting now!"

Captain Billy looked angry. "Ye dare call Captain Billy 'crazy'? Eh? You, a mere boy? Do ye? Crazy?!"

"Yes, Captain, I do!" I shouted at him, panic making me brave. "Uncle Ainsley and I have been trying to keep you out of trouble ever since you got here! We've cooked for you, entertained you, bought you VCR tapes, showed you around, given you a place to stay. *And what have you done in return?* You've burglarized, pickpocketed, threatened people, resisted arrest, and damaged police property. And because of all of this, you've gotten us into BIG trouble! So, yes, I have a perfect right to say that if you go to the meeting, Captain Billy, you are *NUTS!*"

Captain Billy stood there and stared at me. Then he shrugged, "Ye're right, boy," he said. "I *am* nuts. Let's be off."

He took a few strolling steps down the street and turned to me. "You gonna tell me how te get te the meetin'?"

I sighed. I guess there was no stopping him.

I looked at my watch. Eleven forty-five. We'd get there just in time.

But in time for what? I swallowed hard and led Billy downtown.

When we arrived at the Golden Palate, the members of the Ladies' Historical Society and the Men's Lodge were milling around talking to each other. My heart was beating so hard and so fast, it felt as if it would leap into my throat and bounce off my tonsils.

All the men and women turned to look at us as we entered the main dining room. There must've been two hundred of them! And all of them were dressed in their best Sunday clothes, the women wearing expensive-looking jewelry, the men in expensive-looking suits.

"Oh, YOO-hoo!" I heard Mrs. Harkle's voice

before I saw her. She came bustling over with a big smile. "There you are! Oh, I'm so excited! We just can't wait to hear your speech, Professor, oh, I mean Captain Billy. I explained to all of them about what you were doing on the news, that it was just an act to publicize your lecture at the college. By the way, where is your pirate costume?" She was looking at the captain's ankles, sticking out of the sweatpants that were too short for him.

"I hope my uncle remembers it," I said.

Mrs. Harkle looked around the room. "T.J., where *is* your uncle? Is he coming?"

"Yes," I answered.

"Well, you two just come with me and sit at the head table with the president of the Historical Society, Mrs. Thorson. After all, you're our guests of honor!"

Just then, I saw Uncle Ainsley making his way through the crowd, carrying a big grocery bag. I could see a long feather sticking up out of it, so I knew he'd remembered Billy's clothes.

Uncle Ainsley handed the sack to Billy and whispered the directions to the men's room. The captain left, and my uncle looked at me and tried to smile a greeting. But he was just too scared.

A microphone clicked on and Mrs. Thorson's voice boomed out over the loudspeaker, "TEST-

ING, TESTING, ONE, TWO, THREE! OH, THIS IS TOO LOUD," she said, and a restaurant hostess hurried over to turn down the volume.

"Testing, testing, oh, that's much better, thank you. Ladies and gentlemen, will you please be seated. Lunch is about to be served." The members all took their places, and in the confusion, I spotted a familiar head of red hair.

My mouth fell open, and I stood on my toes and peered through the crowd. No, it couldn't be, I thought. She couldn't be here!

Then several people sat down, and I could see clearly. My history teacher, Ms. Dougan, was seating herself at a table near the side door. She looked up, smiled at me, and waved.

I waved back with a sick feeling in the pit of my stomach. That's all I need, I thought. I had hoped no one would know me here, other than Mrs. Harkle.

I whispered a soft prayer that nothing would go wrong, and we would get away fast.

Then, Billy was back, dressed in his pirate clothes, and we sat down at the head table. Mrs. Thorson joined us, along with Mr. Charles Furley, president of the Men's Lodge.

A waitress appeared at our table and announced, "Today you may have your choice of salad or the soup *du jour*, French onion." She nodded at Mrs. Thorson to go first.

"I'd like your lovely French onion soup," Mrs. Thorson said.

"I'll have the soup, too, please," I said, and Uncle Ainsley said he'd have the same.

"Sir?" It was Billy's turn.

"What?" Billy said.

"Which would you like, sir, the soup *du jour* or the salad?" the waitress asked patiently.

"Never heard of a soup dew-zhur," he said, looking confused. "What's a dew-zhur?"

"It's onion, Captain," I said quickly. "I think you'll like it."

"Give it te me, then," he said sourly.

Oh, oh, I thought. I hoped Billy would keep his temper under control today. I'd forgotten to warn him about that, not that it would've done any good.

I noticed that Mrs. Thorson and Mr. Furley looked at each other with raised eyebrows, and Mrs. Harkle suddenly looked a little nervous. Her right cheek started twitching a little up next to her eye.

The captain sat in silence until the soup and salads were served. Then he watched as Mrs. Thorson picked up her soup spoon and dipped it delicately into the warm liquid. He studied her as she tipped the spoon away to scoop up the onion soup, and then raised the spoon to her lips. Billy then picked up his spoon, gripping it the way a pro grips a tennis racket, and filled it with soup. But somewhere between the bowl and his mouth, all the liquid splashed back down in the bowl, on his plate, and the tablecloth. He took no notice of the people at the table, who'd stopped eating to watch him. When another attempt at eating a spoonful of soup resulted in his spilling it in his lap, Billy's patience was obviously used up.

He swore (barely under his breath), and then, as everyone at the table watched in astonishment, Billy tossed his spoon aside, picked up the bowl, threw his head back, and *drank* up the soup, slurping loudly. Then with a thud he lowered the bowl to the table, reached in, and with his huge fingers began to pull strings of cheese and glops of onion out and shove them into his mouth.

To say that the people at our table were grossed out is putting it mildly. Mrs. Thorson looked as if she might faint right there on the spot, and Mr. Furley said, "Well, I never!"

Then came the main course. Chicken *à la* king was served along with green beans and a small slice of canteloupe, with a little sprig of parsley for decoration.

Billy sat waiting for his plate to be put in front of him, holding his fork in one fist and his knife in the other. As soon as he had been served, he dug in and had practically cleaned his plate before anyone else at the table had taken more than a few bites.

Billy looked up, surprised that everyone was watching him again. He smiled and nodded. "Good food, maties." Then he let out the loudest belch I've ever heard in my life.

If you've ever seen that TV commercial where one guy, in a crowded place, starts to tell his friend what his stockbroker says, and the entire room turns and freezes to hear what's being said, well, you get the picture of what happened. Not just our table, but the whole dining room suddenly got quiet, and if eyes had laser beams, Billy would have fried right in his chair.

It slowly dawned on Billy why everyone was staring at him, and he shrugged and said, "Couldn't do nothin' about it."

I won't bore you with the details about the rest of the lunch. It continued to go downhill until all of the courses had been served, all the food was gone, and there wasn't anything Mrs. Thorson could do to put off the speech any longer.

"I guess you'd better introduce him," Mrs. Thorson said to Mrs. Harkle, looking very glum.

Mrs. Harkle slowly stood up and made her way to the podium with the microphone. She switched it on. I noticed her right cheek was still twitching.

"Ahem, excuse me, ladies and gentlemen, but it's time for our speaker. This most, uh, unusual gentleman is an expert on pirate life on the high seas. He has come here today dressed as a pirate of the late seventeenth century, and he *really* plays his part to the hilt, ha ha! He's a visiting professor here in Cedar Springs, and we are, well, we're honored to have him speak to us this afternoon. Ladies and gentlemen, may I present to you Captain Billy."

The applause wasn't exactly thunderous. But Captain Billy stood up at his chair as if Yankee Stadium were giving him a standing ovation. He bowed and waved and held up his hands as if he hadn't expected such a response. Then he turned and swaggered up to the podium.

"Ladies, gentlemen," he said, still bowing and chuckling loudly, "your applaudin' ain't necessary, well, okay, if you want to. Haw, haw." (I think he saw this part on Johnny Carson.)

The strange thing was no one was clapping by this time.

"Standin' before you now is Captain Billy o' the *Midnight Revenge*, one o' the greatest sea cap-

106

tains of all time," he bragged, his voice bellowing into the microphone.

"Stand back a little," someone whispered.

"HUNH?" He looked irritated at being interrupted.

"You're too close to the microphone, Captain," I whispered. "Move your head back from it a little."

"I'll be thankin' ye not te interrupt," Billy barked, but I noticed he moved back slightly.

I peeked through the crowd at Ms. Dougan, who was watching him curiously.

"Me duty at sea is te keep me men in line and take anythin' we kin git our hands on off'n other ships." He looked around the room. "Like food and jewels," and he eyed Mrs. Thorson's pearls around her neck so greedily, that she grabbed hold of them to make sure they stayed there. "And we take money and fine goods."

Suddenly Mrs. Harkle jumped up, her face twitching all over the place, and said, "How about questions? Does anyone have anything to ask the professor before he has to leave? I didn't realize it was so late."

Mrs. Thorson looked at her watch. "Oh, my, yes, it is late at that. Just a few questions."

A man at the back of the room stood up. "What

do you do, Captain, about discipline when your men disobey you?"

I slunk as far down in my seat as I could go.

The captain shrugged. "Either cut off their ear and allow 'em te live, or run 'em through with me sword, cut off their head, and stick it onto a pole at the bow of the ship, as an example te th'others."

Gasps ran through the crowd.

"Captain Billy?" a familiar voice at the side of the room spoke up. *Oh, no, Ms. Dougan!* "Tell us about the famous pirate, Captain Kidd."

Billy's face suddenly turned red with anger. "Captain Kidd?" he bellowed. "That miserable cur, that no good swine!" The audience looked confused and alarmed at his response.

"Kidd's no pirate!" he bellowed. "He's a fake! Any self-respectin' pirate would be *ashamed* of his record! He never wanted to *be* a pirate — he was tricked into it; he started out by capturing French ships for the King of England! He was a bloody GENTLEMAN, he was!"

Billy continued his raving over the gasps and outcries in the dining room. "Don't talk to me about Kidd! He didn't *deserve* that treasure from the *Quedah Merchant!* I nearly had it! I nearly had it!"

The room was in an uproar. "He's crazy! He's not acting! He thinks he's a real pirate!"

"Did you hear him?"

"He's a maniac!"

Then one voice yelled, "Did anyone check his story with the police? Someone call the police!"

That was when I stood up, ran to the podium, grabbed Billy by the wrist, and yelled to Uncle Ainsley to help me. My uncle rushed up and grabbed Billy's arm, and the two of us dragged him away from the microphone and behind the speaker's table.

"Come on!" I yelled. "I saw an exit out back! Captain Billy, you've really done it now. They're going to call the cops!"

The look of anger in Billy's eye was taken over by panic, and he moved along willingly. We ran out a door, down a corridor, and into a side hall way.

We rounded a corner, and came face to face with my history teacher!

"T.J., what in the world is going on?!" Ms. Dougan demanded.

Billy roughly shoved her aside.

Which was a *big* mistake.

"Hi-i-YAH!" In one instant, Ms. Dougan had thrown Captain Billy down on the floor and pressed her foot into his chest.

109

11

She threw me to the floor," Captain Billy mumbled, staring up at Ms. Dougan, astonished. "A *woman!*"

"Okay, T.J., let's have it," Ms. Dougan said, her tiny foot still in the middle of Billy's chest, her hands on her hips. "What's this all about? Are the police looking for this guy?"

"P-Please, Ms. Dougan," I stammered. "Please let him go. I promise I'll explain in school as soon as vacation is over. You probably won't believe me, but I promise to tell you the truth. *Please* let us go."

"Please, Ms. Dougan," said Uncle Ainsley.

Ms. Dougan glanced at my uncle. His hair was all messed up, and his glasses had slid down his nose during the run down the hall. The look in my teacher's eyes softened a little, and she turned back to me.

"Did this pirate, whoever he is, hurt anybody?" she asked me levelly.

"No," I said.

She paused only a moment, then lifted her foot. "Then get out of here," she said, nodding toward the door farther down the hallway, marked EXIT. "I've never liked lynch mobs."

"Thanks, Ms. D!" I said. We helped the captain up off the floor and nearly flew down the hall.

As we reached the exit, we heard voices and footsteps moving into the hall. The people from the lunch were after us!

We pushed Billy out the door, into an alley, and shoved him into Uncle Ainsley's car. Just as we pulled away from the Golden Palate, a police car squealed into the parking lot with lights whirling on top, and came to an abrupt halt in front of the restaurant. We had gotten away just in time.

"Uncle Ainsley!" I said. "I've been thinking about what Billy told us about Captain Kidd and that treasure from the *Quedah Merchant* they were fighting over —"

"I nearly had that treasure," Billy growled.

Uncle Ainsley took a fast turn at Skymore and Pleasant Avenue, and we were all thrown to the side of the car.

"Uncle Ainsley, watch your driving!" I said.

"The cops'll find us in a hurry if they catch you driving like that!"

"Sorry," Uncle Ainsley said. "You're right, my boy." But I noticed he didn't slow down much.

"Billy," I said, "if we could send you back to sixteen ninety-nine to get that treasure, would you tell us where the T.P.S. is?"

"Te git the treasure?" the captain said. "Aye. But that'd be impossible, lad. How d'ye think ye ken find a treasure from three hundred years in the future?"

"Could we do it, Uncle Ainsley?" I asked.

My uncle stared straight ahead of him, studying the road and stroked his chin. "I've been thinking about that same thing, T.J.," he said. "But I'll have to do a little research on it at the library."

"How long will that take?" I asked.

"Maybe an hour," my uncle said. "Think you can entertain Billy and keep him out of sight for that long?"

Up ahead of us was the lake at the edge of Jolly Dan's Amusement Park.

"Stop here, Uncle Ainsley!" I said. "Captain, I know where we can be left completely alone."

Uncle Ainsley stopped the car. Captain Billy changed back into the sweatsuit that Uncle Ainsley had stowed in the car during lunch. Then we got out.

"What're we doin'?" the captain asked.

"We're going sailing!" I said.

The captain looked astounded.

"Call me at home in an hour," my uncle said. "I'll let you know what I find out." He fished some money out of his pocket and handed it to me. "That's for the boat and the phone call."

"Please, Uncle Ainsley," I said. "Just find out what happened to that treasure!"

"I'll do my best," he said, worry lines creasing his forehead. He lowered his voice and whispered, "We've got to get him back to sixteen ninety-nine!"

I patted my uncle's shoulder, then steered Billy toward the boat rental cabin at the edge of the lake. Luckily there was only one other boat in the water this afternoon. We'd have nearly the whole lake to ourselves.

I was a little nervous about Billy walking into the cabin. I thought the guy on duty might recognize him, but we had no choice; he had to come with me. Boats are only rented to people eighteen and over.

The big guy behind the counter didn't even look up when we walked in. He had a little black-and-white TV set in the corner tuned into some soap opera, and he was talking back to the actors.

"Kyle, don't go in there, Kyle," he said to the

handsome actor on the tube. "Victoria and Chantal are in there. They're going to kill you, Kyle."

"Excuse me. We want a sailboat for an hour or so," I said to the guy.

The man stood up and backed over to the counter, keeping his eyes glued to the set.

"That'll be fifteen bucks," the guy said over his shoulder. "No, Kyle, no!"

I put the money on the counter. He threw two life preservers, two paddles, and a key onto the counter.

"Number twelve," he said, still eyeing the TV. "Get out of there, Kyle!"

A shot rang out, a cry came from the TV, and the screen went black, as we left the cabin and headed out onto the dock, to boat number twelve. I tossed in the life jackets and paddles.

"This is the sailin' vessel we're te be takin'?" Billy said, eyeing the sailboat with a funny grin. "It's a wee thing, ain't it?"

"Yep," I said.

I unlocked the chain that secured the boat to the dock.

"You're going to be in charge, Captain," I said as we stepped into the boat. "I've never sailed before."

Billy continued to grin. "No problem, lad."

We pushed off from the dock and paddled out

a bit into the lake. It was a nice day, but here on the lake, the wind was pretty strong. Captain Billy's hair whipped around his head.

"The mainsail is wrapped around the boom," the captain said, pointing to a long piece of metal placed horizontally off the mast in the middle of the boat. It was wrapped with cloth.

Billy took off the elastic cords that were wound around the cloth.

"Raise the mainsail, boy," Billy said, pointing to a rope along the mast.

"This rope?" I asked, touching it.

"Ye don't call it a *rope*, lad," Billy said, rolling his eyes. "It's a *line*. The halyard."

I pulled on it, and the big sail was hoisted up the mast. The wind filled it out immediately and it thwapped hard overhead.

"Wow," I said, looking up at it.

"We'll set it now," Billy said and watched the boom at the bottom of the sail swing suddenly to one side in the wind.

Billy then secured the sail, tying the line to a metal cleat at the back of the boat.

"What's this?" I asked and pointed to a white sheet bunched up at the front of the boat.

"The jib," Billy said.

He pulled on its line, and another sail was raised to the top of the mainmast.

"This is the jib sheet," Billy said, pointing to the line in his hand, "and the winch here takes the strain on the line."

He expertly maneuvered the boat farther into the lake.

I settled back in the boat and tipped my face to the sun. I couldn't believe how peaceful it was. Sailing out there in the quiet tranquility of the lake, I had a hard time believing that we had just, within the last half hour, been the subjects of a wild chase back at the Golden Palate Restaurant. I couldn't quite believe that the police were probably trying to find us at that very minute.

I wondered whether Uncle Ainsley was having any luck researching the Kidd treasure. If only he could find out where the treasure was on a specific date in 1699! We could just send Billy back to that time and place.

If Uncle Ainsley failed in his research, he'd go to jail for sure. We couldn't keep hiding Captain Billy forever.

I looked over at the captain. He didn't exactly look worried about his fate. He faced into the wind with his eyes closed and breathed in deeply, a faint smile on his lips.

"Quite a life, ain't it, boy?" he said. He sighed loudly.

"It's great," I said, grinning at him. "With

116

this strong wind, we're really moving across the lake."

Billy laughed. "You think this is a strong wind, lad? This is a mere whisper of a breeze! Why, I remember a gale in sixteen ninety-four that flattened out yer face! The ship was tossed around like a cork and the wind was so strong and the waves so high, we thought we was all goin' te meet our maker before the day was out." He grinned again, showing the holes in his teeth. "Yessir, that was a day I'll long remember!" He gazed into the distance, thinking about that experience, and smiled once again.

"I'm glad we could go sailing, Captain," I said.

"Aye," he said, shifting his gaze to me. "Me, too, Timothy Joseph," he said.

I checked my watch.

"It's almost time to call Uncle Ainsley," I said, sitting up. "Maybe we'd better head back."

Billy nodded. "Now be careful as I turn us around," he said, releasing what he'd called the jib sheet. "Coming about!" he called out.

"What —?" I started to say.

All at once, I was struck hard on the side of my head and knocked into the lake.

The only thing I remember of the next several minutes was struggling to keep afloat in the water. I'm a pretty good swimmer, but I went under and had to struggle to find the top of the water again. My head was spinning. I choked on the water filling my throat and nose.

I couldn't even yell for help. I coughed, looking around for the boat. I couldn't get my bearings, my head hurt so much.

"Hold on, lad!" I heard the captain shout. His voice sounded as if he were a long distance away. "Hold on, lad! I'm comin'!"

With another cry, he plunged his huge body into the water nearby, sending a massive wave crashing into me. I went under again. And stayed under.

It was so quiet under the water, so peaceful. My mind started to drift off. Maybe I could just go to sleep . . .

A strong arm went around my waist then, and I felt myself being pulled up, up. In a moment, we burst out of the top of the water. Into the sun. Into the fresh air.

I coughed and sputtered again.

"I've got ye, laddie," Billy said over and over, swimming toward the boat. "I've got ye."

Billy got me in the boat, but I don't remember how. In a few minutes, we were at the dock again.

"Are ye ready te join the world agin, lad?" the captain asked softly.

"I think so," I said.

I felt very tired — drained, in fact. But awfully glad to be alive.

I put a hand on Billy's arm. "Hey, thanks, Captain," I said. "You saved my life."

Billy grinned. "And the next time someone says, 'Comin' about,' you better watch yer head. The boom swung out and knocked ye plumb out o' the boat."

"Believe me," I said, rubbing my head and slowly standing up, "I'll remember."

I looked at my watch. My non-waterproof watch.

"I don't know what time it is," I said, "but it must be time to call Uncle Ainsley. Come on, I know where there's a telephone booth."

I was wobbly, but I stepped out of the boat. We returned the life jackets (which would have saved me from nearly drowning if I'd worn mine!), the paddles, and the key. The man behind the counter was now watching a game show and shouting out incorrect answers. He didn't even look up.

Still soaking wet, Billy and I walked to the telephone booth on the other side of the cabin. I dropped in my change.

I heard the phone ring three times before it was picked up. I waited for a "hello" but there was only silence on the line.

Then I heard breathing.

"Uncle Ainsley?" I asked.

"Oh, T.J., my boy!" he exclaimed. "I was so afraid it was someone else! The police were here, but I just didn't answer the door. They must've thought I wasn't here — I did have the foresight to park down the street — and they left. But they'll be back for sure!"

"Did you find out about the treasure?" I asked.

"Oh, yes! Yes, I nearly forgot!" he said. "After Kidd captured the *Quedah Merchant*, he visited a man named Lord John Gardiner on Gardiner's Island, about the first of July in 1699. That's where he buried his treasure chest!"

"So we can send Billy back there!" I cried out. "He can get the treasure!"

Captain Billy's eye lit up.

"Yes, precisely," my uncle said. "Now get home at once! But first, remember, you've got to get Billy to show you where he hid the T.P.S.! Hurry!"

"Right!" I said. "We'll be right home!"

I hung up and turned to the captain. "Come on, Billy," I said. "Let's get that T.P.S. You've got a treasure to dig up!"

Billy grinned. "Follow me, Timothy Joseph!" he said. "There's no time to lose!"

I hustled along with him, around the edge of

the lake, wondering where he could have hidden the T.P.S. "Someplace safe," he had said last night.

Then I saw where we were heading. And it was the most *un*safe place he could've chosen.

Back into the amusement park.

In broad daylight.

Where there were crowds of people.

Where he'd threatened the reporter on TV. And where he'd shot out the tires on the police car.

Terrific.

"You've got to be kidding!" I said. "Captain, we can't go in there. We'll be caught for sure! Everybody'll see you!"

And in fact, as we neared the park, it looked particularly crowded.

"We've got no choice," the captain said.

"They'll stop us at the gate!" I said.

"Who said we'd go in at the gate?" he said, smiling slyly. "I've never been in that way before, boy."

"Oh, no," I said. "I'm not going to break any more laws. I've had enough."

"Then allow Cap'n Billy te get what ye need," Billy said simply. He ran up to the fence, climbed over it, and headed toward the little pirate ship on the pond.

I went to the fence and peered through it.

Which was a mistake. Because just on the other side of the fence was Elizabeth Whitmore.

She eyed Billy curiously. She didn't recognize him at first because he was wearing Uncle Ainsley's sweatsuit. Then she whirled around and saw me. A flash of recognition lit her eyes and she turned back to Billy.

I saw all of this happen, and there wasn't anything I could do about it.

"That's him!" Elizabeth screamed, pointing at Billy as he ran toward the little ship. "That's the pirate from the news, the one who shot out the tires of the patrol car! Call the police! Call my father! Somebody call him!"

People turned to listen to Elizabeth who continued to scream hysterically and point at Billy. They all looked at him, too, then. Many of them recognized Billy and began pointing and screaming right along with Elizabeth. Parents grabbed the hands of their little kids and ran toward the park exits.

"Call the cops!" someone screamed.

"He's dangerous!" someone else hollered.

The park was in chaos.

And Billy kept running.

I watched him, amazed at how fast he could move when he had to. A few people in the park stood and stared after him, looking as if they didn't know whether to run, yell for help, or just watch this crazy-looking character.

Billy reached the ship in just a few seconds and ran up the gangplank. He pulled himself up onto the ship's tall center mast and began to climb.

I was afraid the mast wouldn't hold him. This wasn't, after all, a real pirate ship, but a small replica. And Billy wasn't exactly a skinny little guy.

He kept climbing and the mast creaked, but it held his weight. Up, up, Billy climbed until at last he reached the crow's nest at the top. I saw him reach over the top and grab something from inside the bucket-sized tub and stuff it into the front pouch of his sweatshirt. And slowly, he started back down.

That's when I saw them coming.

Four squad cars squealed into the parking lot at the front of the park. Billy saw them, too, and took a flying leap off the mast, landing with a thud on the deck below.

The police jumped out of their squad car and swarmed toward the ship, and Captain Billy, who was running as fast as his legs could carry him, weaved in and out of the crowd.

"That's him! That's the pirate!" Elizabeth yelled.

"Hold it, pirate! Stop where you are! You're

under arrest!" came a cry from a police bullhorn in the parking lot.

But Billy kept running. He saw me just before he reached the fence. He waved wildly with his arms and bellowed with a big grin on his face, "Get a-goin', kid, I'm right behind ye!"

12

It's amazing how terror can practically turn you into a superhero. I wish someone had clocked my running speed with those policemen tailing us. I know I've never run that fast before and probably never will again. We were tearing up the grass and most likely setting land-speed records as we flew toward home.

I grabbed a quick look behind me at the edge of the park. Two of the cops were chasing us on foot. It obviously had been quite some time since they'd been in tip-top physical shape. They were far behind us. The other policemen had run back to their squad cars and were going to follow us on the street.

Of course, we had no intention of staying on the street. We made it look as if we were going in one direction, and then ducked into backyards and alleys and doubled back toward home. We did this several times to really foul them up, and we lost them after five minutes.

It took us about twenty minutes to reach Uncle Ainsley's. There were no police cars around, but we approached the house with a lot of caution anyway and knocked quietly at the back door.

The door was immediately yanked open, and Uncle Ainsley stood in the doorway. "Oh, I'm so glad to see you! I was so worried! Did you get the T.P.S.?"

"Good as me word," the captain said, and brought it out of his pocket. Now that I could see it up close, it looked like a small kitchen timer with a wooden case around it.

"That's it!" Uncle Ainsley cried and took it out of Billy's hand. "And here are your clothes." Only then did he notice Billy's wet sweatsuit. "Oh, you're soaking wet! What happened?"

Just then, there was a loud banging at the front door, and through the open window, a deep voice shouted, "Open up. It's the police!"

"I'll explain later," I said, grabbing Billy's arm. "We've got to get Billy out of here!"

"Hurry! Hurry!" cried Uncle Ainsley. "Quick, down to the basement!"

The three of us scurried down the steps and into the small room with the time machine. Uncle Ainsley had already turned it on. It was making a humming sound and the door panel was open. Uncle Ainsley and Captain Billy hurried into the chamber while I stood in the doorway, watching.

After inserting the T.P.S. into its hole on the control board Uncle Ainsley said, "Now, Captain, you stand right here on this X," and pointed to a red X painted on the floor. The captain did as he was told.

"Ready," he said, grinning at me.

But suddenly the captain looked startled, as if he'd remembered something. "Wait, Weed. I needs somethin'," and he ran past me, out of the room, and disappeared up the basement stairs. Standing at the bottom of the steps, I could hear the banging on the front door get louder. "Open up in there!" the muffled voice yelled.

"What's Billy doing?" cried Uncle Ainsley.

"I think he chickened out," I said. But just as the words were out of my mouth, Billy's feet appeared on the stairway, and he came lumbering down into the basement.

In his arms he carried a Walkman radio-and-cassette player with earphones and maybe six or eight cassette tapes. I noticed *Rick's Radio and TV* stamped on the side of the machine.

"Me men'll like these," he said, beaming, as he returned to his X on the floor.

"Yes, now we're ready," Uncle Ainsley said, nervously listening to the banging upstairs.

"Hurry!" I said to my uncle.

Uncle Ainsley was obviously very upset. "Let's see now," he said. "I've already set the coordinates for time and place. Billy, you'll travel to Gardiner's Island, July 1, 1699. Here's a map of the island. You'll arrive just before Captain Kidd, so you'll be able to hide and see where he buries the treasure. And then it's all yours. Now let's see, how do I start the transfer?"

"You know," I said. "The rhyme!"

"Oh, yes," he said, scratching his head. "Uh, how did it go? 'Spin the dial around twice, it's cheap at half the price.' No, no, that's wrong. Hmmmmm. 'Push the spot with the dot, for the trip to the ship —' Uh, no. Oh, T.J., my boy, I can't remember it!"

Suddenly there was a tremendous crash upstairs and foot-stomping on the floor above our heads.

A voice boomed out, "Weed, we now have a search warrant. Show us where the pirate is!"

"Quick, Uncle Ainsley! Hurry!" I yelled. "They'll be down here in a second!"

Then, from upstairs, came a shriek. It came from a woman. And a familiar voice wailed, "Oh, officers, I'm so glad you're here! I was just attacked! Oh, it was awful!"

It was the unmistakable high-pitched, nasal voice of Mrs. Harkle.

She continued. "These people, these awful people just broke into my house!"

"Who were they, ma'am?" the police officer asked. "Well, they were — well, they were — gypsies! That's it, a band of roving gypsies! They attacked me and —"

"Come on!" I said to Uncle Ainsley. "Mrs. Harkle's stalling the police! Let's get Billy out of here!"

"Uh, 'pull the ring on the thing and you'll sing like a king.' Oh, T.J., I don't remember!" he moaned.

I put a shaky hand on my uncle's shoulder. "Just relax," I told him. "Just relax and think. Think HARD! It was a great rhyme, Uncle Ainsley."

"Yes, it was, if I do say so myself," he said proudly and seemed to relax a bit.

"Ye can do it, Weed," Billy said and nodded gravely at Uncle Ainsley.

"Okay, you're right," Uncle Ainsley said. "Now let me think. Okay, it was something like this:

Spin this device around twice
for the trip that is nice."

He turned the wheel near him to the right two times.

> "Then pull the rack with a crack
> to track the time back."

Uncle Ainsley reached up and grabbed the wooden rack over his head and pulled with all his strength.

The time machine began to whir and rattle, and it lit up like a telephone switchboard in the old movies. Uncle Ainsley made a few quick adjustments and hurried to join me in the doorway.

"We have five seconds to get out, T.J.," he warned.

I turned my gaze to Captain Billy, that rascal who'd caused us so much trouble and so many headaches. He was standing on his red X, clutching his treasure map, Walkman, and tapes. He looked back at us with a big grin on his face.

" 'Bye, Weed," he said. "Thanks for the adventure. So long, kid. Maybe ye can use this here contraption te visit me some day."

Uncle Ainsley ducked out of the time chamber then, pushing me ahead of him, and, as the door slid closed, I'm sure I saw Captain Billy vanish into thin air.

" 'Bye, Captain Billy," I whispered, and I could feel the sting of tears in my eyes. " 'Bye," I said, a lump in my throat as big as a softball.

I hadn't realized till then just how much I liked our crazy pirate.

13

I sat in my history class and watched Ms. Dougan point out seventeenth-century trade routes on the map. I'd tuned her out about fifteen minutes before, thinking, instead, about Captain Billy and Uncle Ainsley and all that'd happened to us.

I'll always remember the way Captain Billy just dissolved before my eyes as he stood in the time machine chamber.

I didn't have time to think about it at the time, because about two seconds after he vanished, the police came charging down the basement steps. Mrs. Harkle followed right on their heels, still frantically trying to get their attention with that ridiculous story about being attacked by a band of roving gypsies. I guess she knew Uncle Ainsley was in trouble and just wanted to help him. She'll probably never know how much those few extra seconds did help. Looking back on it, I have to laugh about the story she cooked up to tell the police. Roving gypsies! Mrs. Harkle sure has a wild imagination.

But, come to think of it, her story was no wilder than what really happened.

Anyway, the police searched all around the basement and throughout the house, and of course, found nothing. They were suspicious about the time machine, and when they asked Uncle Ainsley about it, he just told them the truth. He said, "Oh, that's the time machine I invented."

One cop rolled his eyes at his partner and twirled his finger around next to his ear as if to say, "Wacko."

The cops questioned me about the incident at Jolly Dan's Amusement Park. I admitted right away that I'd climbed over the fence and that I was very sorry I'd done it, which was true. They gave me a stern warning about that and about consorting with guys who break the law, but they didn't charge me. And since they couldn't find Billy, there wasn't anything else they could do.

The excitement was over now, and Uncle Ainsley was beginning to look relaxed again. He said he'd keep working on the time machine, but he'd be extra careful the next time. I think *he* wants to take a trip next time. It might be less trouble.

I tried to imagine Captain Billy digging up Captain Kidd's treasure. I bet his men loved the Walkman. At least until the batteries ran out.

I'd had a long talk with Ms. Dougan the first day back from vacation. I'd told her the plain, honest truth, every detail of it. She sat there listening with practically no expression on her face the whole time I was explaining. When I finished, she just stared at me a moment. Then she said, "That's the most incredible story I've ever heard. I mean, really amazing."

"I know, it's pretty crazy," I admitted.

"You know, T.J., you should become a writer or a storyteller," she said. "What an imagination." Then she walked away shaking her head.

As I said, all the excitement had died down. I was back at school, back to the routine.

"And now, class, if you'll put aside your notebooks," Ms. Dougan said, interrupting my thoughts as she nodded at me, "T.J. says his extra-credit report is ready, so give him your kind attention. What is your topic, T.J.?"

I stood up and walked to the front of the classroom.

"Pirates," I said. "My report is on pirates and treasures and life on the high seas."

I looked over at Ms. Dougan, and she had a curious smile on her face. The kids were sitting up with interest, especially Elizabeth Whitmore, who hadn't spoken to me since the episode with the police at Jolly Dan's.

"Most of all, my report is on a very special pirate I researched named Billy Mulligrew," I said. "Captain of the *Midnight Revenge*."

About the Author

Carol Gorman was born in Iowa City, Iowa, and now lives in Cedar Rapids with her son, Ben, her husband, Ed, who is also a full-time writer, and their four cats. Ms. Gorman, the author of *Chelsey and the Green-Haired Kid*, as well as several other award-winning books, taught language arts for seven years before resigning to write full time.

APPLE® PAPERBACKS

Pick an Apple and Polish Off Some Great Reading!

NEW APPLE TITLES

☐	MT43356-3	Family Picture Dean Hughes	$2.75
☐	MT41682-0	**Dear Dad, Love Laurie** Susan Beth Pfeffer	$2.75
☐	MT41529-8	**My Sister, the Creep** Candice F. Ransom	$2.75

BESTSELLING APPLE TITLES

☐	MT42709-1	**Christina's Ghost** Betty Ren Wright	$2.75
☐	MT43461-6	**The Dollhouse Murders** Betty Ren Wright	$2.75
☐	MT42319-3	**The Friendship Pact** Susan Beth Pfeffer	$2.75
☐	MT43444-6	**Ghosts Beneath Our Feet** Betty Ren Wright	$2.75
☐	MT40605-1	**Help! I'm a Prisoner in the Library** Eth Clifford	$2.50
☐	MT42193-X	**Leah's Song** Eth Clifford	$2.50
☐	MT43618-X	**Me and Katie (The Pest)** Ann M. Martin	$2.75
☐	MT42883 7	**Sixth Grade Can Really Kill You** Barthe DeClements	$2.75
☐	MT40409-1	**Sixth Grade Secrets** Louis Sachar	$2.75
☐	MT42882-9	**Sixth Grade Sleepover** Eve Bunting	$2.75
☐	MT41732-0	**Too Many Murphys** Colleen O'Shaughnessy McKenna	$2.75
☐	MT41118-7	**Tough-Luck Karen** Johanna Hurwitz	$2.50
☐	MT42326-6	**Veronica the Show-off** Nancy K. Robinson	$2.75

Available wherever you buy books...or use the coupon below.

- -

Scholastic Inc., P.O. Box 7502, 2932 East McCarty Street, Jefferson City, MO 65102

Please send me the books I have checked above. I am enclosing $_____ (please add $2.00 to cover shipping and handling). Send check or money order — no cash or C.O.D. s please.

Name_____

Address_____

City _____ State/Zip _____

Please allow four to six weeks for delivery. Offer good in the U.S.A. only.
Sorry, mail orders are not available to residents of Canada. Prices subject to change.